BLANK CANVAS OF YOU

LAMARTZ BROWN

Copyright © 2026 by Life Lyrics Entertainment. All reserved. No part of this book may be reproduced in any form without permission from the author, except by a reviewer who may quote passages to be printed in a newspaper or magazine.

This book is a work of fiction. Names, characters, businesses, organizations, places, events, and incidents are the product of the Author's imagination or are used fictionally. Any resemblance of actual persons, living or dead, events, or locales are entirely coincidental.

Cover Design: A.Kire Cover 2 Cover
First Edition
Printed in the United States of America
Website: www.lifelyricsentertainment.com
Social Media: https://www.facebook.com/LifeLyricsEntertainment
https://twitter.com/LifeLyricsLLC
https://www.instagram.com/lifelyricsentertainment

CONTENTS

Other titles by Lamartz Brown   v
Connect with me!   vii

1. Mega Dakar   1
2. Mona Lisa Sutton   11
3. Mega Dakar   21
4. Mona Lisa Sutton   30
5. Mega Dakar   41
6. Mona Lisa Sutton   51
7. Mega Dakar   61
8. Mona Lisa Sutton   76
9. Mega Dakar   83
10. Mona Lisa Sutton   92
11. Mega Dakar   104
12. A'shai Blaze   112
13. Mona Lisa Sutton   118
14. Mega Dakar   128
15. Gina Thompson   141
16. Mona Lisa Sutton   151
17. Mega Dakar   160
18. Mona Lisa Sutton   168
19. Mega Dakar   177
20. A'shai Blaze   185
21. Gina Thompson   190
22. Mona Lisa Sutton   194
23. Mega Dakar   198
24. Mona Lisa Sutton   206
25. Mega Dakar   213
26. Mona Lisa Sutton   221
27. Mona Lisa Sutton   227
28. Mega Dakar   233
29. Mona Lisa Sutton   249
30. Mega Dakar   258

31. Mona Lisa Sutton 265
32. Mega Dakar 269
33. A'shai Blaze 273

Blank Canvas of You Spin-Off 277

OTHER TITLES BY LAMARTZ BROWN

Built on Broken Pieces

Damaged By Necessity

Back Down Memory Lane

Sweet Nectar

CONNECT WITH ME!

Website: www.lifelyricsentertainment.com
Join my reading group (The Life Lounge)

Connect with me on Facebook
https://www.facebook.com/LifeLyricsEntertainment

Connect with me on Twitter
https://twitter.com/LifeLyricsLLC

Connect with me on Instagram
https://www.instagram.com/lifelyricsentertainment

Once your reading experience is complete, please be sure to leave a review.

"Yo, I'll break your neck. Keep talking sideways and watch what I do," I said, hating that I had let Tone get under my skin.

"Yeah, alright," he mumbled, knowing damn well he wasn't about that life. I watched as his body slid down the walls of the UPS truck we were in. Today, we were UPS workers, and Ruby scheduled a pickup from this location.

Ruby Rose groomed four boys into men. We were all pieces to the puzzle, to a life we didn't choose, but it chose us. A'shai, Star, and Tone were my brothers, not by blood but by the loyalty we had to survive. By any means necessary, we did what we had to do, and tonight wasn't an exception. What Tone needed to do was remember who he was talking to. He knew better, but I was going to have to show him better than I could tell him.

"This is business. Your feelings not valid. Money over

the corny shit you talkin' 'bout. As I was saying before… we are not here for the cars. We are here to take what's in them." I turned around to face Tone as my eyes pierced through his uneven demeanor. He was on mute.

That's what the fuck I thought. I turned back around and continued.

"This is a big ass garage, so we have to cover all of our bases." I looked at A'shai who was in the driver's seat, and I turned to make sure Star was listening intently. They were never the problem; it was always Tone, who was now looking spaced out.

"You don't think it would be easier to just take the cars and dump them after we get the jewels and diamonds?" Star asked, posing his question differently than how Tone brought it to the surface. He and Tone always made sure to stick together, even when they felt the other was out of pocket.

"I don't even know why we havin' this conversation when Mega said dead it." A'shai blew out a frustrated sigh. "Just shut the fuck up and follow orders. When Ruby puts you in charge, then y'all motherfuckers can do what y'all want. My patience with you niggas is getting thin!" A'shai rubbed his temple as a way to calm himself, which never worked.

We didn't need this energy before a job. Lately, Tone had been disturbing my equilibrium. Something was definitely off about him. We hadn't always seen eye to eye; this was different though. I was going to have a conversation with him. Right now just wasn't the time. We had work to do.

"We must think smart. This gotta go smooth. We about this money or not?" One thing for certain, I knew my brothers were about their money. We wanted for nothing, but that didn't stop us from wanting more. That was what happened when you came from nothing—left for dead, never projected to be anything but a high school dropout or a long-term resident of maximum security.

Being a product of a drug addicted mother and an absent father caused me to get it out the mud. Young, ambitious, and smart, I learned the art of taking what was mine. Meeting Ruby grew the monster inside me. I got my weight up both physically and mentally while in her care. Wandering aimlessly, looking for parental acceptance changed the trajectory of my life.

"Let's make this money." Tone leaned forward, his demeanor not matching the words he spit.

An eerie silence filled the truck as two Dodge Chargers came speeding out of the large garage right past us. I put my game face on. It was show time. It was time to get this money and show these sucka ass niggas what was up. Nothing else mattered in this moment but finishing this job and getting home to some peace and tranquility.

We'd been casin' this chop shop for a few weeks, and we were finally ready to take what would soon be ours. Ruby got word that Pac and Norman were importing rare diamonds and jewelry that would make our accounts that much healthier. We supplied whatever was in demand, and our clients knew they could count on us to get the job done.

Once I cocked my gun, the others followed. That was their way of letting me know they were ready. Star held his fist out to seal our deal as A'shai started the truck. Tone was in his own world, still seated on the floor, now with his AK-47 laying between his legs like he was talking to it. We all got quiet, waiting for him to connect like we always did as brothers before we entered the battlefield.

Tone gathered himself and came to the front of the truck, still not himself but understanding he had no choice. As our fists connected, Star started. "Money."

A'shai followed up with, "Power."

Tone murmured, "Respect."

I finished with, "It's the key to life. So let's use our key." We bumped fists, and A'shai pulled off.

We crept up to the garage door, only to be stopped by security, which wasn't a problem because we were in full character. We had our UPS uniforms on, so we weren't worried. We'd seen this play out for a few weeks now. We hoped we got the same access as the previous delivery guys. A'shai rolled down his window as I sat back in my seat, looking straight ahead. I used one hand to pull the UPS cap down a little lower as I kept my hand on my piece.

"I'm here for a delivery. I have about ten boxes in the back." A'shai changed into another person as he spoke.

"I never seen you before. Where is Chris?" the gorilla-looking security guard mouthed, trying to find answers to questions we were not trying to answer.

"Chris is on vacation, and my boss thought I couldn't do this route by myself, so he sent me with a babysitter." Gorilla Man's eyes landed on me as if for the first time. I didn't even look his way. I kept looking ahead. Not liking the feeling I was getting in my stomach, I had to think quick.

"Partna, I don't care what your boss thought. The point is I don't know you. I gotta check the back before I let you through," Gorilla Man demanded as if he was on to something. He stepped back, waiting for A'shai to get out of the truck to head to the back.

Think quick, Mega, think quick.

My thoughts of what could happen formulated a mile a minute, trying to think of different scenarios. A'shai was trying to buy us time by talking his shit, but by the sounds of it, dude wasn't buying it. I didn't want him to know I moved from my seated position. I moved like a thief in the night as I got up and made my way to the back. Both Star and Tone had their AK-47s pointed at the back door, ready to blast off. We all looked at each other. Sweat was dripping down Star's forehead, Tone was in his fighter stance, and I was thinking about the blood that was about to be shed for the love of money.

We heard commotion outside; something was definitely going down. It was like we were watching shit unfold blindly. We couldn't do anything until A'shai opened the damn back latch. As soon as I was about to run to the front, not caring if we set off alarms, we heard the latch being unlocked. A'shai could hold his own, so I was hoping we were in the clear. If not, we'd make these AKs talk.

"This motherfucker thought he was big enough to eat one of my punches, so I had to knock this nigga out. It was the only way." A'shai stood there with a cocky grin on his face. Gorilla Man was laying on the ground, probably seeing donuts spinning around his head.

"Hurry up and put him back here. We gotta go. Now." Our first problem was solved. I hoped this was our last.

Star, Tone, and I grabbed the security guard, who was knocked out cold. That nigga was heavy, but we were able to roll him inside. We always came prepared, just in case, with a bag that had everything you could think of in it to get the job done. We tied him up and made sure he couldn't talk or scream. Just as we were finishing up with him, A'shai pulled right through the gates. Dude was the only security they had, and by the looks of it, nobody else was on site.

Pac and Norman ran with a small crew from Newark, New Jersey, that got hooked up with some very rich people who had the diamond and jewelry game on lock. After following them for a few weeks, we noticed where they fucked up in their operation. The crew they ran with wasn't allowed at the garage. This was Pac and Norman's safe place, and we came to shake some shit up.

A'shai pulled in, and we waited for the signal that everything was clear. "Yo, we good." That was all we needed to hear. We went right into action.

A'shai met us in the back as we all jumped out. We all looked around, ready to put in this work. There were about twenty-five plus cars in this big ass garage that they turned into a chop shop. We were leaving out of here with something. I threw each one of them a bag and crowbars from the back. Not knowing what cars held what was the only missing piece in our puzzle.

"We got about fifteen minutes to find where everything is at. A'shai, I need you on lookout. Pull the truck back out front just in case we have company. Tone, find the office and see if you can locate some keys. Star, start up front, and I'll take the cars all the way down at the end. Look for things out of the ordinary. It has to be something that stands out about the cars that have the diamonds in them. We'll meet back up here in fifteen minutes."

Each of them took their orders, and we were on our way. We set the timers on our watch for fifteen minutes, and the clock started ticking as we all went our separate ways.

I crept low to the ground, in the back section of the row of cars, walking briskly, ready to crack these doors open. As I got further down, a car alarm went off. It stopped me in my tracks, but there was no turning back now. I stopped at a BMW i8, popped the lock, and once inside, I popped the trunk. It was empty, no traces or residue of illegal activity. I looked from front to back. This was going to be harder than I thought.

I took a minute to think as I got out and looked at the row of cars. Some had for sale signs and others didn't. The BMW didn't have one, so my next thought was to look in a car that had one. You never knew. The ringing of the alarm once I popped open a Honda Civic also sent off another light in my head. *The BMW didn't have an alarm.* I popped the trunk and bingo! There were briefcases with no locks just waiting to be opened. I was almost blinded when I opened the first case.

Vroom! Vroom!

RAT-A-TAT-A-TAT-A-TATAT
Skerrt!

Gunshots could be heard in the distance, but I wasn't leaving here without something, so I hurried and emptied a few cases in my bag and took cover. The car alarms were going off, my heart was pounding, and it made my adrenaline rush. I ducked low, making my way to the front. I didn't hear any more gunshots, but that didn't mean anything. As I got closer, I saw Star on the ground, gasping for air.

"Oh shit! Oh shit! Bro', get up. We gotta go."

He wasn't moving.

The blood that stained his shirt was the first thing I saw when I leaned down to check on him. It was spreading fast. "Talk to me, bro'. Talk to me." If he was trying, I couldn't tell. He wasn't responding.

I tried to locate the wound to apply pressure. I couldn't leave him here alone. He wasn't dead yet, but he was on his way if I didn't get him some help.

"Checkmate! Motherfucker!"

I froze as sweat dripped from my face as I played paramedic. Blood was everywhere, even on my hands that were now high in the air, pleading for my life as the metal piece connected with the back of my head.

"You chose the wrong motherfucker to steal from." Norman's voice echoed throughout the empty space that we occupied. The nigga didn't put any fear in my heart, but I couldn't let him know that, because he had the upper hand.

My focus was on not getting shot, but I couldn't help watching my boy Star bleed out, and there was nothing I could do about it. Star's breathing was slowing down, and his blood was soaking the foundation of the garage we were in.

Where the fuck was Tone?

"Yo, check it. Let me get my boy to the hospital before he dies." It was a terrible attempt at saving Star's life, but it was an attempt, nonetheless.

I slowly tried to get on my feet. The only reason this bitch ass nigga had one up on me was because he caught me in a vulnerable state, trying to keep my family breathing. I couldn't believe I let this nigga catch me slipping. No telling where Tone was. A'shai had to see them come in. Where the hell was he?

I had to think quick on my feet, but he wasn't trying to let me stand. He finally saw the gun that I was trying to hide. He grabbed it, and now I had two guns pointed at the back of my head.

"You think I'm dumb? Don't move until I say move. You're more valuable to me alive, but that won't stop me from sending you to meet your maker. This right here is all mines, and I'll be damned if I let another nigga walk away with it."

"So you're going to let my boy die?" I knew he didn't care. Why should he?

My wheels were turning, trying to figure out a way out of here—preferably alive and on my way to our in-house miracle worker. I had to admit it had never been this bad before.

"I got one of them," Norman said to someone on the

phone, ignoring my question. I knew I could take him, if only I could get on my feet.

Now I was starting to get worried. Maybe they'd killed Tone. Maybe they got to A'shai while he was waiting in the truck. So many thoughts with so little time to think them through. This was bad, really bad. Norman held my life in his hands, and I promised myself I would never let another person rule or ruin my life.

Pop! Pop! Pop!

Gunshots could be heard coming from the outside. It was the distraction I needed. Someone was coming whether it be Tone or Norman's boys. I'd be the one standing when they came through those doors. I spun around just as Norman turned his head to see where the gunshots were coming from. I punched him so hard in his stomach that he folded, and both guns fell a few feet away. I jumped up, ready for war.

He rushed me like a trained wrestler. My elbow met his back as I pounded away, trying to get him to lose his grip. When I saw that wasn't working, I kneed him in his face, confident that I broke something. He stumbled backwards, holding his nose as blood dripped. We both looked for the weapons that fell in our tussle. In our quest to get to the gun first, shots were fired.

Everything went quiet.

MONA LISA SUTTON

"Girl, you look stressed. I keep telling you, you need some dick!"

"I don't know why I hired you." I couldn't help but laugh at my animated friend who was humping the mannequin art fixture that was handcrafted by Artorius Collins.

"You hired me because you know I'm fabulous, and everybody knows that, including you." Gina struck a pose.

She looked cute in her green, slightly baggy one piece, her suede, black, open toe platform heels, and her platinum blonde hair that completed her five-foot-seven frame. My girl was a baddie for sure. She was Eva Marcille's, from *America's Next Top Model*, stunt double, but she hated that comparison.

"Can you believe I was able to book Artorius Collins? This was really a big deal; he's going to bring a lot of attention to the art gallery." I looked around as different staff members were getting the place ready for the showcase.

This was the first time I was able to book a well-known artist to showcase their work in the art gallery. I'd been open now for two months, and we'd had some successful events, but not as big as this one. If this went well, I'd be in the running to host night one of the American Art Collector Gala. Not only did that guarantee me exposure, but it would set me up as a trustworthy partner for future business. This was a lifelong dream of mine that I never got to experience but it was now in arms reach.

"Uh. Duh. Yes, I believe you booked Artorius Collins. Free gifts aren't the only reason I came to work for you. Girl, art is your specialty! You see things that other people don't see when colors are mixed together. You see the inspiration behind the time and effort it takes to be an artist. I came to work for you because you are about to be one of the most successful black-owned art galleries to hit the east coast."

"Well, I got a confession." I tried my best to hold it in, but I had to get it out.

"What? Bitch, spit it out!"

"We are at work; you can't be calling me a bitch in front of the other employees." I was dead serious. We had to draw the line somewhere. That was my home girl and all, but we had to keep it professional when at the gallery.

"Oh my God. Whatever." Gina waved me off, not realizing this wasn't her blog *Girl, Don't Trip* that'd been making noise on the internet. This was real life.

"Anyways… I think Artorius Collins is wack." I waited for her reaction. She looked at me, shaking her head. "What?"

"Girl, I thought you were going to say you got a dick appointment. Tell me something that I don't already know. He's only famous because of who his father is. That and the fact that he's cute. I'll give him some."

"I'm starting to believe you are the one who needs some dick." I whispered *dick* so the rest of the room couldn't hear me.

"I have a list of big, strong men that can scratch my itch, but can you say the same, Miss Honey Boo?" Gina raised an eyebrow and popped her neck. We both burst out laughing.

"Speaking of lists, do you have the updated list of exhibits we are displaying?" We had already finalized the Artorius list. I was talking about the other ten paintings and art fixtures that we would display in addition.

"Yes. I noticed that you took your two paintings off the list. Why?" Gina folded her arms, waiting for an answer I really didn't have.

"I'm not ready yet." I walked away, distracting myself with an area that a couple of staff members were working on.

"Mo, what we not about to do is act like we haven't been talking about this for months. You had time to prepare yourself. You deserve a night of your own, as the featured artist so people can witness you as an artist, not just a lover of art."

What Gina was saying was true. It wasn't that easy for

me, and she knew why. She'd been my friend since we were in elementary school. I wished she would remember the times I had to hide out in her basement when I got inspiration for a piece; the many nights I cried on her shoulder because I missed an art show or wasn't able to submit anything artistic for a placement in a contest I knew I would win, scared that my father would find out; the times I was haunted by the harsh tones of his voice forbidding me to never add paint to a brush let alone a canvas.

My dad never realized how painting made me feel, how the different colors brought together inspired me, how it lifted me when I was at my lowest. All he saw was abandonment, loss, and fear when looking into the eyes of his daughter who was an artist. Not being able to be artistically free was suffocating me. It was causing me to be depressed, and I couldn't live like that anymore. That was why we were now standing in The Picturesque Art Gallery where I was the owner.

"You think my dad will come to this show since it's a big name artist?" I wanted him to see what I'd been up to, but he was still in his feelings that I chose to quit using my degree as a teacher to follow my dreams. Teaching art was fun, but it wasn't what I wanted to do long term.

"Why do you even care, Mona? The cat is already out the bag. You signed your lease; you opened two months ago and haven't looked back. Don't let Mr. Sutton's ole mean behind steal more years of your life. This is the first time you are really living. You're smiling more. The only thing we need to do is get you laid, and you'll be good to go." I promise something was wrong with my friend, but she knew how to make me laugh when it wasn't a laughing matter.

"It's hard not to. I thought if anybody would understand, it would be you." I was done with the conversation. I didn't want to care, but unfortunately, I did. My dad had a way of shutting me out, making me feel lonely. I didn't have too much family outside of him, so it ate me up inside.

"I thought it would be you." Gina mocked me, making me laugh. She could never be serious. "For years, I watched you shy away from a gift that God gave you, only to please your father who needed some healing of his own. I'm not doing that anymore. Your time is now."

"If you say so." I shrugged, only half listening.

"I got it from here. Go pamper yourself. I'll even pay for it if I have to. You haven't really slowed down these past few months, trying to get the gallery open, so treat yourself. You deserve it." Gina was pushing me toward my office, trying to get me to get my things so I could take her up on her offer.

"I miss my dad. Maybe I'll take him out to lunch." I was thinking out loud. I guessed that pissed Gina off.

"I said treat yourself, not get more stressed out talking to your miserable father. I don't know when you are going to learn that misery loves company." Gina sucked her teeth, realizing my mind was made up. "Girl, bye. I'll call you if I need anything." She left my office as I pondered on my thoughts.

I pulled out my phone to call my old man. My father

and I were extremely close growing up. It was always me and him. Some would say I was a daddy's girl, but the way my father had been acting lately, I didn't know. I couldn't wrap my mind around the fact that he wasn't happy for me. He always kept my head in the books, making sure that I was a star student. We really didn't have too many problems until a few months ago.

"Hey, Daddy! What you doing?" I was so excited to hear his voice, which I hadn't heard often this past few months. I always had to call him; he never called me anymore.

"Hey, baby girl. I'm over here putting out fires. These kids will make you think you are too old to be doing this." He blew out an irritated breath.

My dad was a principal at Eastside High School in Paterson, NJ. They called it the famous school because of the movie *Lean On Me*. He had a reputation to uphold. He tried his best to be better than Mr. Clark. Although the school wasn't as bad as in the movie, he still felt he had to go above and beyond to prove a point.

"Let's go to lunch to get your mind off them for a minute. I haven't seen you in like forever." If he was near me, he could see I was pouting.

"I've been busy, baby girl." You could hear papers shuffling and tapping on computer keys.

"I know, so have I. You think you could get away for an hour?" I was persistent. My heart was beating fast waiting for his answer.

"I'll meet you at Mr. G's in like thirty minutes. Baby girl, don't have me waiting. I gotta get back to school. We are getting ready for state testing in May, and I need to make sure things are in order before Spring Break."

"Okay, Daddy. I'll meet you there." With that, we hung up.

I grabbed my keys and my pocketbook then sashayed my way to my car. It was the beginning of April, and the weather didn't know what it wanted to do. I had on some Jiana snakeskin texture, coated ponte knit leggings I got from Fashion To Figure, my flowery printed blouse, and my black Christian Louboutins. You couldn't tell me nothing. *If only I could stay this size.*

I shook the thought from my head, realizing I wasn't two hundred and something pounds anymore. I needed to let that old person die. All I used to do was stress eat. When things got tough, eating was my way of dealing with it. I wasn't that girl anymore. *Or was I?* There was nothing wrong with being a big girl; it just wasn't healthy for me. When I thought of that girl, I thought of depression, anxiety, and low self-esteem. That *wasn't* me anymore.

"Thanks for being on time. You know I gotta get back." I couldn't believe my dad was talking about getting back to school when I had just gotten here. I rolled my eyes, not caring if he saw the irritation on my face.

"Hi to you, too, Daddy. Dang. Let me get in my seat before you talk about leaving already. We just got here."

"You're right, baby girl, I'm sorry. You look good. I

almost didn't recognize you." He got up from the booth and finally embraced me. I melted in his arms.

"Thank you, Daddy. I'm still your baby girl, no matter how I look." I was so used to people from my past staring, trying to figure out if it was really me.

We both slid back in the booth. Although I had an appetite, I knew I wasn't going to eat much due to the possibility of gaining weight. I only wanted to spend time with my dad. Daddy was aging, but he still looked crisp and clean in his suit and tie. Mr. Kurt Sutton was a very handsome man. I always wondered why nobody snatched him up. He now had the house to himself since he basically kicked me out.

"Why are you staring? Is something in my nose?" Daddy lifted his head for me to look up his nose. We were both tickled by his silliness.

"Daddy, you need a girlfriend."

"Where did that come from?" he asked with a raised eyebrow. "You're not lonely in the house by yourself?" I really wanted to know because the first few nights, it was hard for me to sleep, thinking about what my father was going to do all by himself. It had always been me and him.

"No, I'm not. It's peaceful. It's nothing like being able to walk around in your drawers." We both burst out laughing. It was nice to laugh with him for a change. We'd been at each other's throats these last few months. It was no fault of my own; my dad was stubborn and stuck in his ways.

"Spare me the visuals, Dad!" We both laughed at that, on a roll, and I was loving it.

"How have you been, baby girl?" It was a question I was waiting for but wasn't sure if I wanted to answer.

"The art gallery has been doing really well. We are hosting Artorius Collins, a well-known artist who has been very successful." He started fidgeting in his seat, and the energy shifted a little, but not enough to stop, so I kept talking. "Are you ever coming to visit the art gallery?" I asked with pleading eyes.

"I'm busy, Mona." He couldn't even look me in the eyes, which my dad prided himself on doing as a man.

"Too busy to come see your daughter's hard work?" Tears formed at the brim of my eye lids. Crying wouldn't do anything, so I held them at bay.

"I don't know what you want from me. I told you that life is not about nothing. Your career as a teacher would have taken you places."

"How? Daddy, how?" My tone was at an octave I didn't realize until all eyes were on us.

"If you don't lower your voice and stop embarrassing me. Listen, I don't even want to talk about it." His irritation was felt through his words.

"So we are never going to talk about my accomplishments or the great things I'm doing in my life, huh? All because you don't like it?" I guessed this was why Gina didn't want me to come here, but I couldn't give up on my dad like he gave up on me.

"Let's finish our food." I didn't even realize he ordered for me. At this point, I didn't even want to eat.

The rest of our time together was small talk. He ate while I picked through my food. I kept glancing his way, wondering where I went wrong as his daughter. Didn't he want me to be happy? Lately, I'd been asking myself that, wondering how his hate for art and painting trumped my happiness. Up until a few months ago, he was supportive of everything I wanted to do outside of my artistry. We finished up our food and our time was over. What started as a good lunch date didn't end so well, which had me on the edge.

We silently made our way outside to our cars. I was parked behind him, so he didn't have to walk me to my car. I was ready for this awkward tension to be done with. I was eager to see him, but I was happy to be leaving. As we got closer to his car, we noticed someone sitting on it. My dad didn't play about his Lincoln MKG. My eyes grew as big as saucers, realizing that this lady may have put a dent in the hood.

"Mr. Sutton, if I didn't know any better, I would think you were avoiding me." I looked back and forth between the two. I had seen this girl somewhere. I tried scrolling through my memory bank but came up short.

"Get off my car!" was all my dad could muster up while he tried grabbing her off the car.

"You love this car more than you love your kids!" she shouted.

Wait. Huh?

"Daddy, what is she talking about? Kids?" I was his one and only. I was dumbfounded, awaiting his answer.

"Oh, he didn't tell you I was pregnant?"

This had to be a bad dream.

MEGA DAKAR

"Have you lost your fucking mind, dawg?" At this point, I couldn't call him my brother because of the disloyal shit he did that cost our boy his life.

"I did what I had to do to get the job done." Tone knew not to let me get anywhere near him. Once I grabbed ahold of him, I wasn't letting go until there was no more breath in his body. I didn't need a gun; my growing hatred for this clown fueled the blood that would be on my hands.

"I'd run up in your shit; you better thank all these people here. If it wasn't for them paying their respect to Star, I would have smashed your brains in. My time gon' come though." My eyes stalked him, reassuring him that his ass whupping was on the way, especially if he kept it up. He should be apologizing for the sins he committed by going against his family. I gave an order, and I meant what the fuck I said.

A'shai clenched his fist, and his shoulders rolled back. "Make sure I get my turn so I can lay this nigga out, too." A'shai put his dibs in with a murderous stare that I knew all too well.

This was our first time seeing Tone since he left us on the scene. He sped off in one of the cars in the garage; I guessed it had diamonds. Once A'shai peeped Tone speeding off in the car, he ran in, gun blasting. He was there at the right time; bruh saved my life. The only reason Tone's soft ass was standing was off the strength of Ruby.

I hadn't seen profits from said job. The job should have been light work. It was time to re-evaluate and plan my next move. I knew for a fact we weren't fucking with Tone, but I didn't know where that would leave us with Ruby.

There was only so much I was gonna let slide. My time clock was ticking, and I couldn't wait until it went off so I could explode. The walls wouldn't be able to hold us in the room we were in.

"Get off his dick, Shai. He not the only one I answer to." Tone's gangsta was directed at the wrong people.

A'shai jumped up so fast, his feet moved quickly across the room, leaving smoke in the air from his sudden moment. Tone couldn't move quick enough. A'shai's first punch landed, sending a loud thud throughout the room. Tone was trying to catch his balance from stumbling. He tried to swing back, only to miss and shatter the lamp sitting in the back den we were in. Usually, I would intervene; now, I didn't care if he killed him. It should have been him, not Star. I would never wish death on any of my brothers, but that weak shit Tone did was unforgivable.

"Stop it now!" Ruby Rose stood at the door. Her voice echoed authority as the room stopped. All eyes were on her.

Ruby Rose had a way of making four young boys stand at attention when she opened her mouth. Her salt and pepper hair and beige and brown cat framed glasses went well with her five foot-seven stature. Ruby was the mother I never knew; she raised me from a boy to a man. Took me in when I didn't have anywhere to go. She taught us everything about this thing called life.

The slick grin on Tone's face didn't match the blood he was wiping from his mouth. As A'shai punched a hole in the wall, he walked past Ruby into the living room.

"Everybody, get out." A'shai's words rattled the foundation of the house. When people didn't move quick enough, he started throwing them out. We all sat and waited for our privacy. This was a family matter that needed to be handled. A'shai came back quietly on the opposite side of the room, staring at my paintings on the wall, attentively listening.

"We are the keeper of our brother. That's one of the life commandments." Ruby looked around like we cared about that right now. We lost one of our own. Which commandment was that?

"That's not my brother." A'shai's words collided with the wall as he spoke truth, being his authentic self.

"A'shai, who are you talking to like that?" Ruby looked at A'shai as if he'd just lost his mind.

We were all on edge, angry and mad that we got caught slipping. Disrespect was something we didn't tolerate when it came to Ruby. A'shai was a firecracker. He got out of line sometimes, always pulling it in when need be. He looked toward Ruby, empty of thought or emotion. I guessed he couldn't find the words, so I found them for him. In some way, I felt like it was my fault anyway. I should have pulled the plug, seeing how out of line Tone was from the beginning of the job.

"We did as we were told. It's Tone you need to be mad at. He's only living off the strength of you. He better pray to you, like Jesus, that I won't put two in his skull." My eyes watched as the grin that was once on Tone's face disappeared. We never talked this way in front of Ruby. We always waited until she wasn't around to resolve our issues. We were older now and fed up about what transpired and confused altogether why Ruby wasn't lashing out on him.

"Your weapon waits on me to give orders to shoot. Remember that. I'm going to act like this never happened. Remember the commandment. A mother's responsibility is to give you guidance and instruction, and it's your responsibility to follow them. Did we forget?" Ruby looked around the room, knowing damn well we knew the commandment she was referring to. We woke up every day and recited them for years. They were posted everywhere in the house growing up.

The room felt like it was closing in around me. In my mind, I was growing larger and larger, expanding with rage. If I didn't do something fast, to get myself under control, I'd explode and take Tone out, and wouldn't have a second thought about it.

"You keep referring to these commandments that can't bring my brother back. It's funny how you keep overlooking the fact that we did what we were supposed to do. We lost a soldier but still brought you back the diamonds." The red line on my temperature was rising. I couldn't stomach the energy in the air. "We take responsibility for the things we did, but your favorite son over there needs a lesson on loyalty. His greed cost us way more than you are letting on right now."

"We don't divide; we add to the remainder by planning and thinking smarter the next go 'round. Loss is never something we anticipate, but it happened. It should have stayed at the gravesite with Star. I hope I don't have to put another casket on top of him anytime soon." Ruby's blank stare was piercing but had a dark undertone.

"I'm done with all this. It's not worth it. It's not like I need the money. All that you talking only confirms how I've been feeling for a minute. Once we split up this cash, I'm out. When the transgressions of another almost cost me my life, it's time for me to think smarter." I meant what I said. I wasn't putting my life in another man's hands.

"What you saying?" Slow-witted Ruby made her way over to where I was sitting. A'shai and Tone looked on, waiting to see what part of the aftermath they would be on.

"With all due respect, Ruby, I'm not gambling with my life to make money I don't need. Those days are over. We not those poor little boys you found in a park twenty years ago. It's real out there in these streets. I can't help but feel like you low-key telling me something." I stood, towering over her. We did her dirty work, and Tone wasn't built to come into collision with what I had for him. I knew for a fact that A'shai was riding with me.

"You really going to raise up against me? The money you speak of not needing, I provided that. I have a seat at the table which keeps food on yours. What you fail to realize is I gave you your power. I'm the plug, and when you're not connected to me, there's no light." She stood her ground.

I knew my bare hands could slowly drain all the breath in her body from the reality that she lived in. For the first time in my life, I wanted to hurt the one person in the world I thought would always have my back. Ruby did put us on, took us in, but we did the hard part. She secured the jobs, but we provided customer satisfaction. In hindsight, things were not always as they seemed, and Ruby had a way of making sure of that.

"I'm not about to go there with you, Ruby. I don't want to say something I can't take back, and I don't want to do something that I will regret. That's not my style." I pushed past her and tapped my pocket for my keys, slamming the door behind me.

Gutter beginnings made me grind harder to afford the lifestyle I lived now. People said everything happened for a reason; I'd say I was the reason everything happened. Once I understood that commandment, I better understood the assignment. My life was all I had. Everything outside of that, I was numb to. This was the second person close to me I had to bury in my lifetime. I didn't care about many; my circle was tight but dwindling in number. Once seated in my car, I pulled out her picture, replaying that morning in my head.

She was the only one who could calm me down.

"You good, bro'?" A'shai opened the passenger side door of my Audi R8, almost causing me to pull out my gun. I was caught completely off guard, which wasn't like me. I hurried and put the picture away, and A'shai joined me as I pulled off.

Ruby was looking out the window with an expression I couldn't pinpoint but didn't care about.

"Spark that blunt, Shai." We were both caught up in our thoughts.

"Your paintings have a way of calming people," A'shai blurted out.

"You high. Get out of here with all that." We were smoking on some good shit and needed to get our minds off everything else.

"I'm gonna let you be, but you got skills." Between pulls, A'shai got that out. "You really done though?" Never talking about my expiration date with A'shai probably caught him off guard, too. I thought opening the barbershop gave him a sign. I guessed hearing it made it that much more real, and I could hear it in his voice.

"I keep asking myself why we are doing this. Our bank accounts are stacked, we are healthy. What's the point?" These were questions I needed answers to.

"For me, this life is all I know. You know what I'm talented at? Taking shit! It could be your car or your life; it all depends on what the customer ordered." A'shai was spitting some facts. That was that reckless living that not too many people lived through.

"That's not me no more. With the shop just opening, it's time for me to make money in other ways. That means I'll be free to not have to look over my back. To me, the war was won. We lived this long to enjoy the fruits of our labor." Maybe A'shai wasn't to that point yet, but without anybody being there to watch his back, it may cause him to retire earlier than he expected.

"I can dig it," A'shai replied, spaced out.

I pulled into the shopping center where my new barber shop was located. Growing up, I cut all my boys' hair. We couldn't afford it at the time, so I perfected my craft so we could look good for the ladies. What started out as a way to keep us looking fresh turned into a cash business. It took years to realize the skills I possessed, and only after Mya brought the idea to me.

I can't believe she's not here to see it.

I didn't want to go down that rabbit hole, so I turned my car off while A'shai was on his phone. I looked at the sign to the barbershop. *Major Cutz.* I didn't have many reasons to smile, but seeing this caused a feeling of accomplishment to come over me. I was good at something. This was a newly renovated shopping center with different stores, but one caught my eye. The Picturesque Art Gallery.

The doors to the art gallery swung open. The art fixture that made her way out the door caught my attention. She had to be about five feet five. Her curves told me that she was eating well. I shuffled a little in my seat to reposition my shaft. I watched her as she opened a car door, got something out, and walked back into the gallery. My eyes stayed fixated on the door after she was long gone. A part of me wanted to get another glance, but walking into the art gallery would open Pandora's box.

"Yo, I'll catch you later. Try not to let none of this bullshit get to you." A'shai tried to put my mind at rest as he gathered his things before exiting the car.

My mind traveled back to the art gallery. I went against everything I was feeling. I had to see what it was about, or maybe I was trying to get a closer look. Who knew? All I knew was my Alessandro Galet Scritto leather oxford shoes hit the pavement as I bopped my way over to my destination. I wasn't sure what was on the other side of the door, but I would soon find out. I took a deep breath as I opened the doors to the gallery.

MONA LISA SUTTON

His intoxicating scent met me before I was able to lay eyes on him. It hit my nostrils like cupid with an arrow trying to get my attention. My eyes looked over every muscle as his tailor made suit hugged him the way I would if I was his girl. His smooth, almond brown skin looked like it could be featured on a skincare commercial. This man was fine, you hear me? I couldn't help but take a peek at his dick print before mustering up words to speak. "Welcom… welcome to The Picturesque Art Gallery. How can I help you?"

I waited as his tongue met his top and bottom lip so effortlessly. He had my attention now. "Here's some tissue." I wasn't sure why he was giving me tissue, but I gladly accepted. He could give me a spot in those big arms if he wanted to.

"What's this for?" I asked.

"It's for you to wipe that drool off your mouth." His chuckle was so cute. His pearly whites shone as he lit up from a joke I was clearly missing.

"I don't hav…" My mind put two and two together. I threw the tissue he pulled from his suit jacket. He'd definitely caught me slippin'. It had been a minute—that was none of his business though. I couldn't even play mad. That was how much his energy radiated a good time. Guys like him were dangerous, so I had to get away quickly. "We don't open for another two hours. Is there anything I can do for you?"

"I have a few things in mind." His eyes roamed my body, making me shiver and almost cover up. We'd been standing here, and I had yet to learn this extremely handsome stranger's name.

"Excuse me?"

"The things I have in mind, you're not ready for, so let's move past that for now. My name is Mega Dakar, and I'm the owner of the new barbershop, Major Cutz, a few doors down. I wanted to come and introduce myself to the owner. Is he or she in?" I still couldn't move past what he thought I wasn't ready for. Sexy ass Mr. Mega Dakar towered over me, and if I had to guess, he was about six-four to my five-foot-five figure.

"Nice to meet you, Mr. Dakar. My name is Mona Lisa Sutton. I'm the owner of the art gallery." Admiring his big, strong manicured hands, my eyes lingered a little too long. He brought my hand to his lips so my eyes could meet his. Lost in his eyes, I didn't realize how close he was, so close that I could smell the peppermint on his breath. My panties were wet, soaked from his touch, as his juicy pink lips met my skin.

"It's Mega to you. I want to hear you say it correctly. Either you say it now, or you'll be saying it soon, repeatedly." Mega let go of my hand, his cockiness making me cream. Usually, men like Mega turned me off. It was something about this one, though, that I couldn't put my finger on.

I called his bluff. "Mr. Dakar, it was really nice to meet you. I have things I have to attend to. If you ever need anything, us black business owners have to stick together. I want to congratulate you on opening up what I'm sure will be a successful business, black man. I'm proud of you." The shops at Riverside in Hackensack, NJ, had always been home to the white privileged and influential people that had a portfolio. Over the years, it had changed a little, but I was happy we were bringing some flavor to the area.

"Wow. Thank you. You are the first person, outside of my brother, who has said that to me." The spark in his eyes told a story that he overcame some things. Our black men didn't get praised enough.

"I also see you want to learn the hard way. You'll be saying my name; don't worry." There was that smile again. He looked around, almost hesitating, like he knew he did something wrong. He quickly focused his attention back on me. "You have a dope spot here."

"Thank you! Art has always been important to me. Unfortunately, I couldn't show how important it was to me until recently." I couldn't believe I was about to tell this man my whole life story.

Shut up, Mona.

"Friday night, I'm going to pick you up and take you out to celebrate you for finally following your dreams. I'll pick you up here at eight p.m., and wear something nice."

Leveling out my breathing, I began to gain control. "I don't… I don't go out on dates with guys I don't know."

"I thought that's how you get to know guys you don't know."

"Thanks for the invitation, but I have to pass. Right now, my focus is on my business, and I can't afford for anyone to get in the way of that." I really didn't believe the words that I spoke, I had to think quick.

"Pleasure is my specialty for the right person, so be careful what you ask for. Get out your head and start experiencing life, Mo. All work and no play, you know what that means." I hadn't been called Mo in forever. My mom used to call me Mo when I was younger. It was like the name was banned when she left.

"You still there? Did I say something wrong?"

It took a minute for my brain to catch up with my words. "You didn't say anything wrong. I was just thinking about somebody, or should I say something." Thinking about my mother always opened up a portal to the unknown, and I couldn't unravel in front of my company. "I'm a super busy person, Mr. Dakar. I'll have to take a rain check."

"Nah, I'm not letting you get off that easy. How about I bring you lunch, and we can work our way up to a date?" He was persistent. I looked him over once more, loving the energy he brought to the surface.

"We can do that." I didn't want to sound desperate, so I tried to hide my excitement.

"Good choice. I was going to come in here every day to ask you until you said yes, so it didn't matter." We both enjoyed that laugh. Mega took my hand once more, planted another kiss, then proceeded to the door. "You're stuck with me now. Enjoy the rest of your day, beautiful." With that, he was gone.

I had to sit down and process all of this. I kept looking at the door, seeing if he would return. A part of me was super excited, and the other part of me was nervous as hell. I hadn't gone on a date in years. I rushed to my office and dialed the one person I knew would talk me off the ledge.

"Hey, girl." Heavy breathing could be heard in the background.

"You are not going to believe this."

"What? You got the American Art Collector Gala bid… I know it has to do with… business because your life is so boring." I checked my phone to make sure I wasn't losing signal.

"Whatever! No, I'm still waiting on word, but that won't probably be until after the Artious show."

"Ummm… O… kay… What is it?" Gina's voice was low and raspy.

"Are you working out or something?"

"Yes, bitch, damn." I tried to block out the sounds of echoing pleasure, giving my friend the benefit of doubt that she wouldn't answer the phone if she was indeed doing what I thought she was. "Anyways, I have a date." I jumped up and down in my office chair, not sure why I was excited. All I could hear was heavy breathing, so the line wasn't dead.

"Sssss, ssss!" I looked at the phone, almost in disbelief at what I hoped I wasn't hearing.

"I told you not to answer it, but you ain't want to listen." A deep baritone voice interrupted what I thought was a conversation.

"Girl... I'm gonna... have toooo... to call you... back!" Gina didn't even wait for me to collect words. I couldn't even front; I was a little jealous that she was getting her back blown out and here I was excited about a man possibly noticing me. We were not the same. Obviously, she was winning in life. If Mr. Dakar acted right, I might have to see what was under that suit.

His smell still lingered somehow. He left more than just his scent; he left a good first impression.

Outside of my dad and Gina, of course, life didn't allow much room for relationships. I secluded myself from the masses, never confident in who I was, searching for an identity behind a little girl lost. I stood from my desk and looked in my large, full-body mirror that Gina insisted I should have. At one point in my life, I didn't like the person looking back at me. My weight kept me imprisoned from knowing my worth.

My dad tried his best to build my self-esteem. What he didn't know was that a mother's love was needed, although he was doing the best he could. I often wondered what my mom would look like. Those memories were tucked away in the attic of our house. I had to sneak to look at pictures of the lady whose face I stole. A five-year-old could only remember so much. My vision was blurry, thinking of all the moments where I needed her to tell me it was going to be okay.

"You look beautiful, baby girl."

I didn't even look my dad's way as I tugged at the silver dress that no longer looked right on my body. Gina's mom, Mrs. Thompson, did her best helping me pick out my dress for the eighth-grade dance. Bad enough nobody wanted to take me. Gina didn't know I knew she turned down Tyrone's invitation to be his date. She lied saying no one asked her, either.

"Chubby girls shouldn't wear dresses stuck to them like gum under a park bench." I could still hear the boys at the lunch table laughing at Malik's hurtful words. He must have been speaking for the rest of the boys because nobody spoke up to defend me. My hand stung from the smack I lit his face up with after his amateur comedy joke. Gina had no problem following up with a smack of her own.

I was hoping that we got suspended and couldn't go to the dance. As luck would have it, my dad talked with Principal Fulmore and got him to let me attend. He felt as though community service was a better punishment. I wish he would have talked it over with me first. Now, here I was, looking like a shiny whale. Malik would sure have a laugh at my expense.

"I don't wanna go." I stomped to my bed and sat on the edge, looking down at the beige carpet, mad at the single tear that escaped my watery eyes. It got away before I could gain control of my feelings. Mrs. Thompson was nice enough to do my makeup. If I didn't get a grip, it would have been for nothing.

"Baby girl, I wish I could fill whatever void you are feeling. I can only keep reassuring you that you are royalty. You're perfect, and you'll be perfect for whoever God has for you. Loving yourself will make a world of a difference when you look through the lens of love and authentic existence."

"Do you think she would think I look beautiful?" She couldn't look through the lens of love due to her many years of neglect. I was afraid to say her name sometimes, but he knew who I was talking about.

"Your mother would think you were one of God's most beautiful creations. You look just like her." Finally able to lift my head, I saw as his eyes turned dark. They always did when you mentioned Geneva Sutton or whatever she went by these days. I didn't even know if she had died. I was only left with the story my dad told me.

"Her love lens must have gotten lost with the lens of a mother, in a dark room waiting for the pictures to develop."

I descended from my large canopy bed, determined to prove to my mother that I didn't need her to be pretty. I didn't know where it came from, but that extra boost of confidence made it a little easier. I gathered myself and got ready to face my apprehension and push through the best way I knew how to.

"Fine, I'll go." It was obvious by my movement to get ready. Gina arrived, and our limousine took us to The "NEW" La Neve's Banquets in Halendon, NJ.

"Jamel said I better save him the last dance." Gina

rolled her eyes, flashing a smile, knowing damn well she was loving the attention Jamel was giving her.

"That's so he could rub on your booty with his nasty self." I stuck my finger in my mouth, pretending to force myself to throw up.

"You better let Terrell feel on your butt." That boy didn't even talk; I doubted if he even knew what to do with his hands.

I wanted to get the night over with. That didn't stop me from hiding in the limo once I saw what everybody else had on. Gina almost had to drag me out by the tail of my dress. All eyes were on me as we met up with a few girls from our school. They were more Gina's friends than mine, but they weren't mean, so I tolerated the up and down looks they gave me. One thing I knew, I wasn't ugly. If only I could stop eating, affirming what my young thirteen-year-old mind equated with beauty.

The school dance was jumping. We danced, laughed, and I forgot about all my earlier meltdowns. Malik kept his distance; he was still eyeing me every time I did look his way. Jamel and Terrell were rocking with us the whole night. You would have thought we were on a double date. Terrell did shock me with his dance moves. I was actually impressed. He still didn't talk much when we were on a break from dancing. Gina, Jamel, and I carried the conversation.

"I'm about to go get me something to drink. Y'all want something?" I was parched from hitting the chicken head and chicken noodle soup dances.

"I'll go with you." Terrell finally spoke up.

"Good, y'all go so I can talk Gina into giving me a kiss tonight." Jamel's hormones were on full display.

"Ewww... nasty!" I headed toward the drink table to get some punch. Terrell followed behind me, trying to keep up with my pace. "Why are boys so nasty?" I handed Terrell a cup of punch as I took a sip from the cup I grabbed for myself. He chuckled a little. All night, I was trying to stay away from the snack table. Why did it have to be so close to the drink table? I eyed the different pastries they had, cookies, and the other goodies that lined the table. As soon as I bit into the chocolate chip cookie, Malik took it upon himself to knock it out of my hand. His shoulder collided with mine, catching me completely off guard.

"Aye, man, what you doing?" Terrell stuck his feet out to trip Malik, causing him to fall face first into the punch and drinks table, sending red liquid all over the floor of this fine establishment. Even with the music blasting, everyone turned to see what the commotion was. Most of them laughed once they noticed what had happened, the others trying to piece together the mystery. That night I saw Terrell in a different light. So much so that we were inseparable from that day forward. Entering high school as a couple, making him my first and only experience.

I didn't have a healthy representation of what a woman should look for in a man. My dad was a great example, but he never brought a woman around. I only knew his love for me; I didn't get to witness him in love. I only witnessed the heartbreak of the way my mother left him.

Left us.

Not only didn't I have a mother to teach me about beauty and class, she also wasn't there to help me identify the red flags in relationships. It would've saved me a lot of embarrassment if I would have seen the signs that Terrell was gay. I had our whole life planned out when he had a different plan all along. So many years later, it still stung. Mr. Dakar might just be the person to remove the stinger.

B<small>ANG</small>! Bang! Bang!

Loud knocks could be heard coming from the front of my luxury loft condo. In my line of work, you didn't know who it was. It could be your enemy, or it could be the pigs, but either way, I was prepared. My hand met the metal piece, smearing a little paint as I gripped Ether. That was what I named my roommate, my gun of choice for this situation. There were many more strategically placed throughout the loft. Today, Ether would do the honors.

My footsteps were silent as I made my way to the front door. I waited for movement as I listened, pressing my ears to the cold surface.

"Who is it?" My back met the door as I held my gun in the air, waiting for an answer.

"Yo, open the door, with your paranoid ass." A'shai was

pounding on the door and was talking shit while doing so. I flipped the lock, opened the door, and put the safety back on my gun.

"I bet you your ass was in here moving like a ninja. Relax. Noman and Pac ain't alive to knock, and their boys ain't gangsta enough to go against Godzilla and King Kong." The sinister crooked smile of A'shai displayed his ruthlessness. A'shai believed every word he said, and I couldn't agree more. I still wasn't willing to get caught slippin' though.

"Shut yo' ass up!"

I forgot I told A'shai to come through so we could rap about what was next. We still hadn't gotten our cut from Ruby from the chop shop job. We were still laying low. There was no communication with Ruby. It was time to pay her a visit. It wasn't about the money, although it was our money to have. I wasn't sweating it too much, but if Ruby wanted me to even consider doing business with her, she needed to come correct.

I thought back to one of the commandments: *Honor thy Leader so Life Can Be Long.* We were brainwashed to idolize Ruby, who we thought had the power to nurture lost souls like myself.

"You heard from Ruby?"

Grabbing water out of the refrigerator, A'shai sat his big ass on my counter, ignoring the seats at the table or the island where I was seated. Not realizing it until he caught the dry and somber tone of my voice as I spoke words that Mya would often utter to A'shai. "Man, get off my counter and come to the back room." I walked off, leaving that thought right in the kitchen.

"My bad." He wanted to say more but thought against it. There were so many memories all three of us shared in this very place. I swear, A'shai did things just to get on Mya's nerves. She was his little sister, though. He looked out for her even when they were at each other's necks. They had a different type of relationship. I knew it still hurt that she wasn't here. I would have been out of the game sooner if Mya wouldn't have abandoned me, leaving me to figure this all out by myself without the love and support of my soulmate.

"Ruby's been calling me, but I haven't been answering." I took a seat on my stool, getting in position to finish the painting I'd been engrossed in for the past few hours. I'd been inspired by Mo, the Black queen who was following a dream I never had the courage to. Her thick thighs, plump pink lips, and eyes that seemed familiar kept playing in my head. I couldn't take my mind off her, so I released it the only way I could.

Oftentimes, I wondered if I was ready to open myself back up after the loss I encountered unexpectedly. It was crazy how one day you could be with somebody, and the next, they were gone. That was a different type of disappointment.

"She knows not to call me. I ain't making no moves without you." Loyalty wasn't just a word for A'shai. It was a lifestyle.

"Ruby better pay up." Money was owed, and I wasn't

about to let it slide. She should be giving us Tone's half. "I think it's time, bro'. I want to focus on the shop." The tip of my brush stopped outlining the frame of this piece I was working on.

This conversation came sooner than I thought. We had another job lined up to do some work for Gavino Contini, a grimy Italian cat we did some contract work for a few years back. I really didn't care for him, but that was one of the biggest paydays of my career. Maybe it was a sign not to even bother.

"I wish you would have told me this before so I could have prepared. I ain't even mad at you, though." A'shai's body became rigid, not defensive but emotionless.

"You right. I assumed you saw the moves I was making. I thought that would have made you think about what was next for you." I laid the paint brush down. I had to realize all we knew was how to take; life took from us, so we knew firsthand the impact it could have.

"Can you do this last job? It will set me up to transition to whatever I'm about to be doing." He shrugged his shoulders, unsure of what was on the other side of not knowing the real meaning of why we were here.

A'shai wasn't begging, but it was a plea to hear him out. With Star gone and Tone out of the picture, we had to build a plan for a two-man team. We had to do the job of two people to equal a team of four. It was doable for sure. I didn't know if I was willing to put money into the pockets of someone I couldn't totally trust. It wasn't about me, though. I couldn't leave A'shai hanging. Ruby's finder's fee wasn't going to be her normal payout now that I was completely handling everything.

The dark night glowed. The streetlights came alive with the passing of each block as the tires of my cocaine white Range Rover cruised to the destination. My eyes were low from the sativa of Blue Dream hitting my lungs. My large frame exited the Range as my Alexander McQueens hit the pavement, making my way up to the compound that was Ruby's house. Ruby lived in a brick front manor cul de sac in Ridgewood, NJ, tucked far away from her other lifestyle, almost as if it was another world. Blood brought the bricks that held this place she called home together.

    I had my own key, but not knowing where we stood, I chose not to let myself in. Ruby always shot first and asked questions later. At least that was what she taught us. Not that she had to, but she proved herself on more than one occasion, although we did the heavy lifting. The doorbell could be heard from outside the house. Ruby knew I was here before I had a chance to put my car in park. I waited at the door, realizing for the first time I may now be an outsider to the one who raised me.

    "Mega, to what do I owe this pleasure?" The front door slowly opened. Ruby's devilish grin would be considered a smile if I didn't know her.

    My legs wouldn't move as I stared at the materfamilias. Her energy didn't match the disposition of her black and white polka dot blouse, black leather pants, and Christian

Louboutins. Her cat eyed glasses always added a touch of attitude and a wink of charm. If you didn't know better, it would get you sucked in and manipulated. I always admired how she was the bait, and we were the fishermen.

"May I come in?" We didn't break eye contact. Ruby opened the door wider to allow me entrance. Without words, we proceed to the living room.

"You want something to drink?" I took a seat on the red leather curved sectional, taking in the room like I hadn't spent countless hours and days in this very spot. At this point, I didn't trust her to make me anything. With me, once trust was tested without a clear vindication, the person moved to another compartment of my brain. I had to compartmentalize to protect the murderous nature that comes from love and loyalty.

"Nah, I'm straight." Without a word, she made her way to her destination as I continued to look around. Ruby was quiet, which she never was. Her voice was always loud, even in the room of peril.

I zeroed in on a picture of myself and Mya when I first brought her home. Ruby couldn't stand the thought of another female in her house. Mya didn't care. She held onto me tight as I brought her into my world. Eventually, Ruby warmed up to her. By then, we had moved out the house.

My stomach sank. I would never hear her laugh or smile again.

"How have you been doing, Mega?" My attention was diverted to the double old-fashioned glass in the center of Ruby's hand that housed her brown liquor. My guess was it was Crown Royal XR whiskey filled to the top, which was more than a shot. Ruby took a seat on the opposite end of the sectional, but not so far that I couldn't smell the liquor on her breath.

"Do you really care, or was that your way of breaking the ice?" I wasn't in the mood for games or even small talk. Ruby's poker face remained intact as she took a sip from her cup. A soulless stare stalked me before she opened up her mouth to speak.

"I don't know where I went wrong with you. I'm not the enemy, and until you see that, nothing I say to you is going to matter."

She was correct in saying that, but she still had some explaining to do. The only reason this conversation was even happening was off the strength of A'shai.

"It's always been me calling the shots when we are on the job. You were always wise counsel, but it was me who made sure nobody died."

The blood that drained from Star's body came from the hands of Tone. If Ruby continued to sit here and not acknowledge her wrongs, she was the one who held the gun. That was how I saw it.

"Mega, baby, I know you're hurting. You and Star were close." I couldn't let her finish whatever it was she was going to say after.

"I'm not a little kid anymore, Ruby; it ain't working with me. Keep Tone away from me. You better hope A'shai doesn't see him. What happened to all the loyalty, honor, brotherhood, and family shit you preached all these years?" I leaned up for her to really hear me. "I see you differently. You ain't living up to the shit you drilled into our heads. That shit is crazy watching it all unfold in front of me."

Ruby had always been someone who was raw and unfiltered. She ruled with an iron fist, with rules and commandments, oftentimes gifting us with what we thought were the finer things in life. It was a step up from the group homes A'shai and I were accustomed to. We did what we were told and got rewarded with money, trips, cars, and anything a young boy could dream of, all this time not realizing we did it ourselves.

"You're grieving, so your mind is clouded right now." Ruby's long, black, pointy fingernails gripped her glass, taking back every drop of the brown liquor as if it was iced tea. "Gavino thinks highly of you. He wants to meet with you to go over the plans for the next job." Ruby got down to business. After this, I didn't have to deal with her, so I backed off just a little.

"You better tell Gavino he better come wit' that money. I'm not doing no petty job. It's been some years since we worked with him. My price went up. We top tier, and we not taking no shorts."

I stood to my feet, watching Ruby watch me as I ended the conversation.

"Wait, I have something for you. Give me a minute." Ruby moved throughout the house on a search to find who I thought she really was.

At one point in my life, I used to love to hear those words. After every gift, there was something I had to do to earn it. I never saw it like that until life had a way of slowing me down. I started peeping stuff after Mya died; a lot of shit started to become clearer. People wanted you to do what they wanted you to do. When you went against that, they had no choice but to show who they really were. It hit different when it was family. When it was someone you loved.

"I apologize for having you waiting." Ruby approached me with a black Louis Vuitton duffel bag. "This is for you and A'shai from the last job." When Ruby handed me the bag, her phone dropped, screen shattering on impact. "Damn!" she yelled.

"How much is in here?" Her phone wasn't my problem.

"It's a hundred grand—fifty for you and fifty for A'shai." I wondered how much Tone got. It didn't matter at this point; his bitch ass was going to get what was coming to him.

"I'm going to trust that this money was distributed right." Ruby stopped looking at her phone long enough to bring her attention back to this conversation. Her eyes squinted behind her frames, almost examining me.

"I'll let you know the date, time, and location once confirmed with Gavino. You can let yourself out, Mr. Dakar." Ruby's wide grin and downturned eyebrows didn't match the tone of her words.

I never stayed in a place where I was not welcomed. I knew when I was being dismissed. I didn't want to be here anymore than she wanted me to be. I prepared myself for the rain that was now pouring once I opened the door. Loud raindrops hit the side of the duffel bag as I hurried to the truck, making sure not to step in a puddle. I popped the trunk, almost to a dry place.

Pop! Pop! Pop!

Gunshots rang off as I ducked behind the Range, taking cover. I was seconds away from being exposed if they would have let me get to my trunk. I swiftly pulled my gun out and started letting the bullets fly as I targeted the getaway vehicle. Heart racing, blood boiling, and confirmation that I hadn't been hit had me jump in the truck on my way to a safer place to think this through.

MONA LISA SUTTON

"Girl, why is this fine man asking for you like he knows you?" Gina ran up in my office like someone was chasing her.

"If you weren't getting your back blown out, you would have known." I didn't have time to deal with Gina's antics. It was now or never. My heart rate sped up, not believing this was really about to happen. I immediately got up to fix myself in the mirror.

"If I knew this mystery person was tall and sexy, I would have given you a little more of my attention." Gina hurried to my side to help me get right for Mr. Dakar.

"Is that right? The way you were breathing says something different. I hope that nut was worth ignoring your best friend." We both chuckled.

"I got more than a nut. Mr. Golden Pipe had my legs

shaking and had me calling Jesus himself." Gina stopped to fan herself, reminiscing about that very moment.

"Eww... you're nasty, and I don't want you to embarrass me, so I hope you're on your way out." I looked myself over in the full-length mirror, trying to gain the confidence to get this lunch date over with that I shouldn't have agreed to. The black wrap around blouse, red leather skirt, and black ankle boots felt like a good choice this morning, but now I was second guessing myself.

What if he doesn't like what I have on? I do look a little fat today.

Even with me turning down the bacon, egg, and cheese sandwich that Gina ordered me this morning, it did nothing to ease my mind.

"Uh-uhhh... Don't be acting brand new because you got a dick appointment, finally." Gina playfully rolled her neck, laughing. "You look fine, girl. Let's go before he thinks you ran away or that we're back here plotting to kill him or something." Gina grabbed her things as we made our way to the front.

The walk from my office to the front of the gallery seemed like I was walking the green mile. If I had an alter ego this was the time for me to transform into character. As Mr. Dakar came into view, his eyes fixated on me with a look I couldn't place. This man had a dozen red roses waiting for me. I almost tripped over my two left feet but recovered well.

"We don't know you like that, so don't try anything crazy, or I'm going to be all over your ass. You hear me?" Gina was dead serious, looking up at this perfectly structured man like he wouldn't be able to kill us with his big, manicured hands. That didn't stop her from giving him the cutthroat gesture like she was the Undertaker. I was so embarrassed. He got a kick out of it though.

"Shawty, trust me. Your homegirl is in good hands." The way he chuckled and licked his succulent, pink, plump lips had my mind in a trance. He did it so effortlessly.

"He's gonna be trouble." Gina tried her best to whisper. She gave me a hug before proceeding to the door.

"Excuse my friend; she didn't have her meds today." My heart was beating out of my chest as he approached me.

"Can I get a hug, since you're giving out hugs?" Mr. Dakar handed me the roses, waiting to see if I'd take him up on his offer.

I hesitated. He was so close that it was almost impossible not to get wrapped up in his embrace. I shook my head yes. I closed my eyes, enjoying his defined muscles, the way he smelled, and the fact that I felt protected. My head rested on his toned abs; that was how much taller he was than me. I could have stayed here forever, but he let go to gather the items he brought for our lunch as I watched him closely. He wore a black Hugo Boss T-shirt with some black Ralph Lauren slim fitted jeans, topping it off with some classic Pradas. It had to be a crime for this man to look the way he did.

I bet he is too good to be true.

"Lead the way, Mo Love." I liked the sound of that. It rolled off his tongue like he had been calling me that forever. The large picnic basket he carried was created for an outside picnic, so I wasn't sure what he had in mind. The small breakroom wasn't made for that type of mood.

"This is our breakroom. It's not much, but it's where my employees come to take breaks from all the hard work they put in." He looked around.

"I'll be right back. Stay here." He vanished back into the gallery before I could utter a word. *Did he leave something?* I sat down with so many thoughts running through my head. This gave me some time to get my girl caught up on the happenings.

ME:
> He has me waiting in the breakroom, what if he doesn't come back?

GINA:
> Do I need to come back with my taser and tase his ass to death?

ME:
> Lol. No stupid. I'm nervous, what if he thinks I'm fat and took all the food back?

GINA:
> Mo, don't do that to yourself, you're beautiful and any man will be lucky to have you.

ME:
> You're my friend, of course you would say that.

"Smile for me. Your smile is contagious." I didn't even sense his presence as he stood in the doorway watching me. I hurried and put my phone away.

"Where did you go?" I was curious; he no longer had the picnic basket. My worst nightmare was coming true. *He did think I was fat.*

"Follow me." He grabbed my hand, leading me back into the gallery. I couldn't believe my eyes as we made our way to a candlelit picnic setup in the middle of the gallery floor. My hands covered my mouth, looking at the knitted blanket placed on the floor with pillows, fruit, and a variety of foods to eat. He'd outdone himself on what I saw before me. It was perfect. The candles were placed in a circle. All we had to do was step through and take a seat.

"Oh my God, I love it." I slowly spoke, not believing he did all of this for me.

"That breakroom was killing my vibe. We needed to be amongst the art that gives us peace. I want you to relax. If you are like me, the paintings and art fixtures will loosen you up."

"That is something we both have in common. Thanks for doing this." I got comfortable on the pillows, looking at the spread before me. Mega was such a gentleman. He handed me a lap cloth to cover up. I guess he didn't want a sneak peek of my black lace hip hugger panties. It wasn't a good day to have a skirt on, but we worked around that.

"I wasn't sure what you wanted for lunch, so I grabbed a little of everything." That, he did.

"I'm not hungry," I quickly replied.

"Don't be shy, Mo Love. You can eat in front of me. I'll even feed you if you want me to." Mega grabbed a pineapple and held it up to my mouth. I willingly opened up as the juices agreed with my taste buds. I loved pineapples.

"Why do you keep looking at me like that?" His dark brown eyes enticed me.

"You look familiar, like I saw you before... maybe in another lifetime." He paused, shrugging it off. "Why are you just now showing the world how important art is to you?"

"You're going right in, huh?" I was stalling for time by asking a question to his question. I didn't know if I wanted to open that door. I wasn't sure where it would lead.

"I'll go first. Art had to take a back seat. It didn't put food on my table. I had people depending on me." His eyes grew darker at that revelation.

"So you're an artist?" I was intrigued. "I mean, I know you cut hair—that's an art all in itself. Like, do you paint?" I waited patiently for him to find his next words.

"I wouldn't say I'm an artist, but I do love to paint. Every time I get the inspiration to actually do something with it, something always happens to make me put it back down." His words were ice cold, almost as if he had to pull it from the freezer of his heart.

"Do you think I'll be able to see some of your work one day?"

"If you act right, I might let you into my world, but not until you tell me a little bit about the famous Black art gallery owner." I got it. He wanted the spotlight off of him.

"Umm... I was forbidden to even say the word art, let alone show my skills of the talent that my girl Gina said

God gave me." I looked down, no longer making eye contact. It was easier to do so when he was pouring out.

"I know that had to be hard." Mega moved closer, his energy letting me know this was a safe place. "What made you take your dreams back from the thief who stole your innocence?"

What a way to put it.

"Everybody was living their life, happy, while I cried each and every day, getting up and going to a job that I hated. I loved the impact I had on my kids, the potential to cultivate new artists so young. It wasn't until one of my twelfth graders got me right." I was happy to be laughing to keep from crying. "She said to me, 'Ms. Sutton, you need a life 'cause this ain't it.' Man, I remember that thing like it was yesterday."

"Why do you think at that moment it clicked?" My pillow now became Mega's pillow as he sat beside me. He was a giant to my small figure. I wanted so badly to lay my head on his chest and take in his invigorating scent that I couldn't seem to get out of my shop from our first encounter.

"My student Eva marched to the beat of her own drum. I always admired her courage to do whatever she wanted to do with no limits. She was who I wanted and needed to be when I was her age, but I cared about my dad's feelings over mine." I looked upward and disparagingly shook my head, trying to hold back the tears.

Mega allowed me to hear his heartbeat as he wrapped his solid arms around me. His heartbeat created a melody to a song of soothing for my wounded soul. It actually stopped the tears from flowing. Never in a million years did I think I would be here. These past few months had been an eye opener. Clearly, I was missing out on what could have been my life if I would have lived for me and not everyone else.

"I'm so sorry, Mega." I pulled away to plead my case.

"See, I told you you'll be calling me Mega soon."

I chuckled, resting in a place that felt familiar. I couldn't believe this was really happening to me. This was a peace that I could not buy. I was hoping this was real. I lowkey felt like I was in a movie watching something blossoming right before the viewers' eyes. The only difference, this time, I was the leading lady, and my supporting castmate was doing his job. As much as I didn't want to leave his arms, it was time to run my lines.

"Who are you, and where did you come from?" I was a little nervous in asking, but it was a legit question.

Mega shifted on his pillow a little.

"I'm not the FBI. You don't have to worry," I said, and that made him smile.

"Meek said it best. Gangstas move in silence, and I'm not sure if you ready to know the real me. I'm from the bottom, and my goal is to stay at the top by any means." Mega stared at the Jean Micheal Basquiat painting that was a part of the Neo-expressionism movement. The way Mega said it sent chills up my body. I watched him closely as he took in the painting.

"Every gangsta has a story, and something tells me yours is intriguing. Did you always want to be an entrepreneur?"

"Nah, I just always wanted to survive."

I now had Mega's attention. His focus shifted to me. "I guess we all had to survive something as a kid. It's crazy that our childhood shapes us into who we are today. We should have been having fun while our parents took on that responsibility. It wasn't fair to us; nobody told them to have us." I was trying my hardest not to get angry for the millionth time.

"My parents were the streets I walked at night. It was up to me how I made it to the next day. It was that way for a long time until someone saw something in me that helped change what my life could have been." Mega ran his fingers through my silk press, massaging my scalp. Gina would have a fit if she was here. There was always time to get my hair done though. I closed my eyes because this shit felt good.

"Was it a girlfriend who helped you?" Mega stopped rubbing at that question. My eyes popped open to see what happened.

"Blood don't make people family. Let's just say I created my family because the one that God gave me was too selfish to accept such a blessing." The seriousness in his tone showed a side of him that he probably didn't ever expose.

"Sometimes I wish I could create my family. Don't get me wrong. Gina is my best friend and sister for life. I would have picked a different mother though. Maybe that would have made my father act differently." Build-A-Bear wouldn't have nothing on the family I would have built if I could have.

"Sometimes, even the ones you choose can turn on you, so it's not as dreamy as we'd imagine. I learned that a long time ago." Mega was making sense, but you could tell it was from a dark place. It was a layer of him that was almost pulled back. It was a peek into the man seated next to me.

"You can't win for losing, huh?" I looked at Mega, realizing that life was going to be what it was going to be.

"You know how I win? I do what I want, when I want, and how I want and make sure the people connected to me are good. That's winning to me." I wasn't mad at all. Mega knew how to use his words.

"Let me find out you a barber by day and a gangsta philosopher at night." Mega was giving me a gangsta lecture.

"I do whatever is necessary to live the life I want." Mega was speaking his truth.

"Did you guys get all that? I think we got him." I pulled at my shirt like I had a mic on.

"Yeah, aight." He grabbed me up as we both laughed, then leaned in and kissed my lips with such passion that I got dizzy and drifted into ecstasy.

His lips were so soft and moist, causing the hair to stand up on the back of my neck. Electricity shot through my body as we explored each other's mouths with our tongues, enjoying the arousal of the sexual tension that came from our connection. His lips felt so good pressed up against mine. It had me wondering what those lips would do to my clit if I gave him the opportunity.

WHAT THE HELL *am I doing?*

I sat back in my office chair and reflected on how far I'd come.

This was uncharted territory. I never thought I would be feeling this way about anybody after Mya. It was only recently that I was able to even say her name without going into this dark place. I still had issues sleeping. On some days, I didn't even know how I was functioning, let alone running a successful business. I still couldn't shake the feeling that I was doing something wrong by thinking of someone else.

When I was around Mo, she brought something out of me that I had locked in a vault. I was painting again and looking forward to our next encounter. With everything that had happened within the past few months, none of it mattered when I was with her. It was like she created a different world, and it was just me and her in it. How she managed to do that, I would never know. What I did know was I couldn't get her off my mind.

"Yo, what you doing back here? You better not be beatin' ya meat." A'shai burst through my office door on a mission to irk my nerves.

"Next time, knock before you come in here, playa. I'm gonna have Ether waiting for your ass." I laid my Sig Sauer P320 on my desk for emphasis. We locked eyes and laughed.

"Oh, I'm so scared," A'shai said in the most cinematic voice he could conjure up. If people only knew how funny he was. Most people never saw this side of him. He was always stone faced and ready for war. At times, I wondered how he got pussy. If I didn't hear him in the next room deep in some gushy, growing up, I would think he had desert dick.

"What you want, yo? I'm on my way out." I stood from my seat and started to gather my items of choice, still hoping this was a good idea.

"Where you going?" A'shai looked on with a confused expression as I gathered the art supplies I brought for a special somebody.

"My nigga, I'm grown." I knew he meant well, but I wasn't sure he was ready for me to move on. I didn't even know if I was ready to move on. I was going with the flow. Mya was his little sister, and he took that title seriously. He always said if he ever fell in love, he wanted what we had. Although he felt it wasn't in the cards for him, he always made sure to say it to me.

He eyed me suspiciously with a raised eyebrow. I hadn't painted consistently in years, and for him to see me with paint and art supplies, had to have his wheels turning. If we didn't have so much going on when he showed up at my condo a few weeks ago, we would have definitely talked about my newfound... I didn't even know what to call her.

"Nah, we not changing how we move. Let me know what's good wit' you, bro'." We promised ourselves as youngins to always keep each other in the loop, even when we felt the other wouldn't like what we had to say, just in case shit popped off.

"It's this shorty who caught my eye and got me doing things out of my norm, fam," I said, holding up the supplies.

"Oh, word? I was wondering when your romantic ass was going to find somebody." There was a genuine but weak smile that plastered across his face.

"You don't think it's too soon? She was my fiancée, A." I finally let the thought leave my lips. I'd been thinking about it but never said it out loud.

"Dawg, Mya been gone." He paused, took a deep breath, and continued. "She's been gone for three years now. She would want you to be happy." The tone of A'shai's voice let me know he meant what he said.

We'd barely talked about Mya since she went to sleep and never woke back up. A'shai and I had an understanding when it came to losing Mya. It was still a tough topic. You could see that we were healing if we were able to talk about it. Maybe this was my sign that it was time. The hurt and agony we experienced would probably never go away. With that in mind, we couldn't stay stuck on what could have been. One thing for sure, I knew Mya was proud of my accomplishments. She always wanted me to leave the street life alone, and I finally made it to the exit.

"I don't know if happiness is in the cards for me just yet. This girl though, she… she lights up my dark surroundings. Her smile is contagious, bro'. It's something about her that seems familiar, though. It's like I saw her before; I can't put my finger on it." It was still a mystery, one I was willing to solve if Mona let me.

"I gotta meet her if she makes you feel soft and cuddly again." A'shai laughed. "Damn, you all open and shit. Did you even hit yet?" he wanted to know.

"It ain't even about that. You know how much pussy I can get? This shit different." I shook my head, realizing I was in deep with someone I really didn't know.

"Yeah, yeah. I know my brother, and I bet money you've been thinking about how wet her pussy is. It may not be your first thought, but I guarantee it's your second." We both laughed. That was all the confirmation he was going to get about that.

"Real quick, before you go skipping to love land. I've been keeping my ears to the streets about the opps shooting at you. Somehow, whoever crossed that line went ghost. We gonna find them, and you won't have to look over your shoulder, bro'. I know you want this new life, but we can't let that slide, or we'll regret it."

There was a little hurt in A'shai's voice when he said that last part. I knew he was still processing my exit, so I didn't take it personally. I'd been so focused on the shop and now Mo that I forgot to help him find what was next for him. I couldn't leave him hanging like our parents did or sacrifice him like Ruby did. I made a mental note to start investing money and resources to find something for A'shai to do. I didn't trust the streets without me watching his back.

"Good lookin' out. Let me know when you get that intel, and we'll handle our handle." I knew A'shai enough to know he wasn't going to let it go, so I had to ride this one out. He was doing it for me, for the respect we built in these streets.

"Money," A'shai mouthed.

"Power," I followed up.

"Respect," A'shai echoed.

"Is the key to life," I finished.

"Yo, grab the rest of this stuff and walk with me down to the art gallery." We were closing for the night. It had been a great day. We'd been getting a lot of referrals, so business had really picked up.

"Yooo, I peeped that joint when I pulled up. That's where shawty works?" A'shai was intrigued.

"She's the owner," I said proudly.

"No shit. That's like a match made in heaven. So, she's the reason you got your mojo back and started painting?" Before I had a chance to respond, he kept going. "Yeah, nigga. She got you in a chokehold and you don't even know it." A'shai thought he had it all figured out.

"Man, shut your ass up." I laughed. There might be

some truth in what he was saying, but I wasn't entertaining him.

"Damn, they say milk does a body good, but what type of milk y'all drinkin'? That shit gotta be from Wakanda." Mona's animated friend joined us as her eyes lustfully landed on A'shai.

"I can show you how to keep your vitamin D levels up," A'shai mouthed off with a grin.

"I bet you will… Mona! Girl, you didn't tell me he had a friend!" Mona's friend yelled while walking off in a hurry to the back. That got a chuckle out of both of us.

"Bro', you didn't tell me she had a friend." A'shai looked at me, rubbing his hands together. "She talks too much, but I got something to shut her up." I couldn't hold in my laugh, knowing he was dead serious. A'shai loved a good challenge.

"I wanted you to see for yourse—"

I stopped mid-sentence. I had to take in her beauty. Ms. Mona Lisa Sutton lit up the room with her rich caramel skin. Her lips were glossed, ready to be kissed again, while her body called out for me to save it. I gravitated to her; it was like my feet had a mind of their own. In my dreams, I couldn't wait to hold her in my arms again, so I wasted no time. That kiss did something to me that I couldn't quite explain and didn't want to explain until I knew for myself.

Nothing else mattered as we embraced.

"Let me see if your arms make me melt like that. Your

arms are so big and strong." Mona's homegirl used her finger to outline A'shai's body. She rested her head on his chest and she wrapped herself in his arms.

"Damn, girl, I get it!"

"Please excuse my friend." Mona left my embrace to snatch her friend up. A'shai and I made eye contact, loving the entertainment.

"Let's not excuse the fact that you haven't officially introduced me to the man that's been stalking you."

"The only thing that needs to be stalked is that pussy. If you had the right nigga dickin' you down, you wouldn't be worried about what they got going on." No filter A'shai let it be known without a care in the world. "As a matter of fact, go get your stuff so I can walk you out. Let's leave these grown adults alone so they can enjoy their night. If you act right, we might just enjoy ours." A'shai smacked ol' girl on her ass and followed her to the back.

"What is all of this?" We focused back on the reason I was here. Mona's eyes lit up, trying to piece together my existence. I was lost in her beauty. The way she wore her natural curly hair had me rearranging the heavy artillery below my belt. I was a gentleman, but my other head had different thoughts. I didn't know if I would be able to keep my hands off her. My hand met hers, locking our hands together. I was owed this moment. It was time for me to be open to possibilities.

"I want to see you in your element, while we listen to some dope ass music and have a few drinks. Is that alright wit' you? You down to hang with me tonight?" My questioning was rhetorical, and her soft chuckle confirmed she knew just that.

"I'm putting on my playlist. Nobody is listening to your shoot 'em up, bang bang songs. Let me help you with some of these bags." While I was thankful for her asking, she was going to find out what type of man I was.

"I don't know what lames you've been with that you let waste your time, but I ain't them. I got this." I grabbed the bags and my setup for tonight.

"Let me go check on these fools. They've been back there a little too long for my liking."

A smirk spread across her face, probably realizing that her friend might be bent over. Knowing A'shai, it was a strong possibility. Her hips kept me in a trance as her four-inch red bottoms glided across the floor. I walked to where I wanted to set up and got to work, getting caught up in my thoughts.

When you started living, you looked back at all the times you weren't, as a reminder to enjoy the unknown. You didn't know where it might lead you. For three years, my focus was getting money and taking all my anger out on the targets that were in my path. There was a lot of bloodshed in the name of making money. On the flip side of that, it was my therapy for losing my lifetime partner. I was a wanderer, lost, searching for a peace that I could not buy.

"This is so cute!" Mona's excitement sent a chill through my body.

I think I finally found it.

"I want to see you create in real time. Tonight is about

you, me, and the brush strokes on the canvas. You might even get a two-step out of me as a bonus for spending some time with ya boy." I took her in as she admired the paint, the brushes, and the whole setup. When I painted, it had always been me and my thoughts. Mya always left me to do what I did, knowing that I needed that time.

"I think Gina is right. You're going to be trouble. The way you keep looking at me and this Hennessy tells me she may be right." Mona held up the gallon of that Henn Dog.

"That's for me. I got you some Bartenura Moscato. That's all you, Mo Love. Leave that brown liquor for someone who can handle it." I towered over her, gripping the bottle, pulling her close to me. Mona's gaze almost had me kiss her lips, willing to risk it all. It was more that we had to learn about one another.

I took hold of the bottle of Henny and poured my glass. The wine glass I filled to the middle, not knowing Mona's limit. It was now time to show her that my playlist was more than rap songs. I walked up on Mona as she was getting her supplies together for our night of limitless potential.

"Here you go, Mo Love." I handed over her drink of the night.

"I want to take a shot with you. One thing you're gonna learn about me... I can handle my own." She put her glass of wine down and held out her hand for my glass. "As a matter of fact, bring that whole bottle over here, Mr. Dakar." I saw she was trying to be funny. I wondered who would have the last laugh.

I grabbed another glass and poured myself some of that

brown. I never measured. It was most definitely more than a shot. The glass that Mona was holding wasn't lacking either. This night was getting more interesting. We could barely stay apart now, so I knew when that liquor got up in us, it was gonna be a different story. I held up my glass for a toast, and Mona followed suit.

"To tonight and us being free to allow our minds to drift to rhapsody." Our glasses met, and neither of us left a drop. "Oh, here is the first song off my playlist." I had plugged my phone up to the gallery speaker, and I pushed play on my Apple Watch.

The best song wasn't the single, but you weren't either
Livin' in Ladera Heights, the black Beverly Hills

Frank Ocean's "Sweet Life" blared through the speakers. Mona sang along, ecstatic at my song choice.

Keepin' it surreal, whatever you like

Whatever feels good, whatever takes you mountain high

Mona grabbed the Henny and poured her some more. She wasn't heavy handed like me, but she had a shot. She even became my bartender and poured some in my glass. I didn't mind it, but I hoped she knew what she was doing. We took our seats in front of our canvases. We looked at each other, and without instruction let our brushes do the talkin'. Frank finished singing about the grapevines, mangoes, peaches, and limes—a sweet life—before Mona and I started buildin'.

"Does a sweet life exist in real life?" The blue from my paint brush stopped blending the colors together on the canvas. I really considered her question. Although I may not have thought of it that way, it had been a similar deliberation.

"I learned at an early age that life is what you make it. It's all in your control." The music for the night shifted to Tems "Avoid Things."

"Control is something I never had. My father was pulling the strings to my life. I didn't see a problem with it until I wanted to do something I liked. It crushed me to the core of my being when he didn't show up to the opening of the gallery." Tears tried to escape her beautiful eyes.

"You took that control back. You are now living your dream. No matter how long it took you to get here, at least you got here."

"A part of me still feels like he has control. I still long for his approval. I still want to hear him say that he is proud of me. He used to say it all the time. I feel like I left him for art like my mom did, and that's a hurt I wouldn't dare inflict." I stood up from my stool, and her back met my chest as I wrapped her into me.

"You're not what your mother did. It's time for you to stop doing her time. You were acquitted a long time ago. Walk in that freedom." The playlist understood the assignment. Snoh Aalegra's "In Your Eyes" blared through the air particles as I turned Mona around to face me so I could look into her eyes.

Not only was I met with her eyes, her lips invited me in for a moment of fulfillment. I picked her up, palming her phatty in my hands. Her arms were encased around my neck as our tongues got to know each other. The shots of Henny combined our intake, getting us drunk off each other's taste. I knew she felt how brick I was, and I couldn't wait to feel how wet I knew she was.

"You better stop kissing me like… this… Mega!" Mona released her leg from around me, breaking our connection. She reached for my shirt, pulling it up for me to take off. Her small stature didn't allow her to make it past my shoulders. Her small hands tugged at my tank top, and that came off without a problem.

"If you want to see me naked, just say it." I licked my lips, calling her bluff.

Lust peeked over the horizon of self-doubt, illuminating the need to continue. Mona took a step back. She looked me over, at war with her mind and the rivers flooding between her nature's valley. I'd give her something to look at. I loosened my belt, my manz bustin' to get free. My pants were off, and my socks came off with them. I was standing there in my briefs.

Mona's eyes grew wider.

"If you want to show me your dick, just say it." She built up the nerve to challenge me.

In seconds, my briefs were lying next to the rest of my clothes. I grabbed my dick. It didn't need a stroke; it was already standing at attention. I tapped my thickness in the palm of my left hand. Mona looked on, squirming like the girl from *The Five Heartbeats*. I made my way over to her, kissing her on impact. Before you knew it, she was out of her clothes, and our skin met with an urgency. The wall became our support.

I wanted to kiss her other lips. I wanted to taste that freestone of her nectarine, the sweetness of her juices flowing into the tunnel of my mouth. I lifted her eye level, holding her against the wall. Without warning, I lifted her higher, wrapping her legs around my shoulders.

"Wait... Wait... I'm too heavy. I don't want to hurt you." I paid her plea no mind.

My tongue rested at the opening of her hidden treasure. Her soft hands held on to the crown of my head as I breathed in her anatomy. Her apprehension dissipated once I got through the gates that held the key to her soul. The tip of my tongue circled her inner workings. The moans that left Mona's mouth had me working overtime.

"Mega, what are you doing to me... Boyyyy!"

I answered her by feasting off the waves of her ocean.

"Oh my God! Mega... don't drop me... I'm cumminnnn'." Mona gripped my head tighter as she poured me a drink from her fountain. I licked it all up. I wasn't through with her yet. I lowered her down, making sure not to drop her like she asked.

"Can I make you cum again?" I lowered my head to suck on her nipples. I took turns, being sure not to make the other mad. They both needed my wet tongue for them to grow.

"You can do whatever you like, and that ain't the liquor talking, either."

"I know. That's that pussy talking. I woke it up and now it wants my undivided attention," I said confidently, knowing what my tongue could do. "Turn around and bend over so my manz can have a conversation with that pussy." Mona's hands met the wall like she was about to get patted down by the police. I wasn't the police, but I had a baton as my regulator.

I took my time coating my shaft in her wetness, slapping it against her clit.

"Meggaaa, keep doing that... please."

"I'll keep doing whatever you like, Mo Love." I didn't know how long I would be able to though. I wanted to fill her up with slow strokes, but first, she had to get used to my size.

Mona gasped, scratching the wall once the base of my dick entered the promise land. My strokes were calculated so it wouldn't hurt too much. Pleasure was my specialty, and having a big dick could be a gift and a curse. I was glad I was given the gift to have a woman respond with the many orgasms they were guaranteed.

I was finally all in and ready to pick up the pace.

"Yessss, boy! You really deep in that shit. I think you in my stomach." Loud moans echoed through the gallery one after the other. Our bodies started smacking to the rhythm of the beat of the music. Silk Sonic's "After Last Night" was our soundtrack for this moment. I kept going, even after Mona came twice, back-to back.

"You throwin' that shit back now, huh?"

"Just like you got good dick, I got good pussy."

"You damn right you do." I smacked her right booty cheek.

"I want you to cum with me this time... Mega... please cum with me!"

"I got you, Mo Love. I got you."

She was throwing it back in a circle.

"Mega!" Mona yelled.

"I know… I feel you." Between the grip she had on my dick and the way she rotated her hips to meet my pelvis had my knees buckling.

Our release together had both of us out of breath and struggling to stand. I pulled out, and Mona turned around and slid down the wall to the floor. I followed suit and sat right next to her, resting my head on the wall. We were both spent, trying to recollect ourselves from the mountain we'd just come off, allowing our heart rate to decrease from the marathon we'd just run. My head shot to the paintings that we started but never finished.

"Let's each create a piece to showcase here in the art gallery?" Mona had skills, and if it took me to challenge her to get her to see it, I was down to show my skills as well. She gathered her composure and looked toward the easels.

"I don't know, Mega. This was fun and all, but I'm not ready for all that yet."

"You have three months to come up with something. In those three months, I'll show you just how dope you are by giving you some inspiration. He's one of them." I pointed to my dick, jumping at the thought of another round.

"That's enough motivation right there." She giggled, climbing on top of me.

MONA LISA SUTTON

I HAD an extra pep in my step as my heels hit the concrete of the driveway of the house I grew up in. I almost used my key but quickly talked myself out of that thought. My dad had been living this secret life, and I didn't want to walk in on him enjoying that. I rang the doorbell as I stood on the porch taking in the Sunday afternoon air. The house I grew up in was not too far from the art gallery in Teaneck, NJ. I still couldn't wrap my mind around the fact that my dad had to pass the gallery every day to get home. He never took that detour to come check me out.

It was officially spring, and the sun was setting, but the nice weather did nothing to calm my nerves. These days when in my father's presence, I was always on edge, not sure what could trigger his hate and dislike for me. Lately, he had me thinking that he got someone else pregnant because he no longer loved me. He hadn't denied the accusations which made me believe it was true. I started to look at my dad differently already; this just totally changed my view of the first man I ever loved.

"Baby girl, why didn't you use your key?" my dad asked, opening the front door.

You know why.

I wanted to be bold and say it, but I didn't want to ruin our time together.

"It smells good in here, Daddy." I missed his home-cooked meals, something he got better at as time went on. When my mom first left, all we did was eat fast food. It was one of the reasons I think I had gained so much weight. The fat jokes started coming in by the dozen. It wasn't until we came back from the doctor's office that he cared enough to try and do something about it.

"I haven't cooked dinner since you left and moved on with your life." I followed him into the kitchen after taking my shoes off, leaving them by the front door.

"You kicked me out, remember? Awww… do you miss me?" I went over to him while he was stirring what looked to be cabbage. I wrapped my hands around his waist for a quick hug.

"We are not going to go there." Mr. Kurt Sutton put a stop to that conversation. This was when I saw him through the lens of his government name. This wasn't my dad talking. I had to learn the difference. It was the only way to keep me coming around.

I took a seat on the island stool. Flashbacks of Mega invading my space populated in my mind. It was a reminder of what he did to my body; it sent chills up and down my spine. I crossed my legs to silence the urge of calling Mr. Dakar's number to set up another appointment. I knew he was booked and busy, but I was premium clientele, so I was sure he would have changed his schedule to come rearrange my guts.

"Are you cold?" My dad looked on as I tried not to shiver again from the thoughts of Mega's thick meat.

"No, I'm good. What's something that made you smile this week, Daddy?" I needed the attention off of me.

"Something that made me smile?" He thought about it for a few seconds. "I saved a bunch of money on my car insurance by switching to Geico." We both couldn't control our laughs.

"Daddy, I'm serious," I let out through giggles.

"I woke up this morning. That made me smile," he quickly replied.

"That's enough to make anybody smile. Millions didn't make it, but we were one of the ones who did," I said proudly.

"True… What's something that made you smile today, baby girl?"

I was on the fence of what my answer would be. I had a lot to smile about these days. There were two things that brought me joy and had me cheesing like a fat girl in a candy store. The gallery was one, and Mr. Dakar was another. I knew where the conversation would head if I said something about the gallery, so I chose the latter. I still didn't understand what Mega and I were doing, but it felt so right.

"I met someone," I blurted out and folded my hands on the island before me.

My dad's eyebrows arched at my declaration.

"What you mean you met someone?" my dad probed.

It was weird saying it out loud, so I understood his confusion. The only guy my dad met was Terrell, aka Terrella if you nasty. He saw firsthand what that relationship did to me. My dad would have gone to jail if I hadn't stopped him from sending Terrell to meet his maker. I looked on, debating if I should proceed. Then the view of Mega's toned muscles, sexy lips, and his heavy dick invaded the cloud above my head.

"I met him… I met him while working. We've been on two dates." They were unofficial dates, but my dad didn't need to know that. "I think I like him, Daddy."

My dad's piercing eyes stalked me, searching for the words to deliver his point. That made me a little nervous. When Kurt Sutton had something to say, he would just say it. It was when he calculated his words that you should worry. That always meant that he was about to spit some fire to your ass. My dad needed anger management and maybe even some therapy, but he refused to get well. He was a good person; he just had to get the past off his back.

"I hope you checked his credentials. We don't need another repeat of you down in the dumps like that rump ranger had you the last time." My dad knew I hated when he called Terrell a rump ranger. Yes, he was gay, but he didn't have to keep reminding me. Terrell cheated, and that was what ended our relationship, not who he cheated with.

"I'm getting to know him." That was all I could muster up.

"I hope so. You still haven't told me his name."

"His name is Mega Dakar, and he owns the barbershop a few doors down from the art gallery." I hoped the word art didn't trigger my dad. I mentally prepared myself just in case.

"He's a business owner. That's a plus." He paused. "If he makes you happy, baby girl, you have my blessings."

"He is really a sweet guy. He loves painting just as much as I do." Damn, the words slipped right out my mouth without me even realizing.

The energy completely shifted once I spilled those beans. My dad's eyes grew darker as he threw the kitchen towel on the island before me.

"What did I tell you about dating an artist?"

"He paints and paints really well, but he is more focused on his barbershop." Mega wasn't a full-time artist, so I didn't see the big deal.

"You a hoe just like your mother, chasing after these low-life dreamers, thinking he can fulfill a void. He only wants one thing, and that's to manipulate you into opening your legs. That's what artists do—they break up happy homes. Them jokers think they can do, say, and have anything they want."

"You just said if he made me happy, you would give me your blessing." My anger levels were rising. I started to see red.

"That's before I knew he was a rolling stone. I forbid you to see him. Don't be like your mother and choose a life of destruction over a relationship with your dad." He slammed my plate of food on the island, almost breaking the fine China that had the thin fried pork chop, white rice, and cabbage with cornbread.

There were many nights I cried, locked up in my room, hating myself, thinking about losing my mother. I didn't even know if she was dead; I never got that closure. My father had taken on that responsibility. He continued to break my heart and show me why my mother probably left in the first place. One day he was going to learn to love without conditions. I wasn't the same little girl anymore, and he was about to find out.

"You have a lot of nerve!" I flipped over the plate.

Crash!

The plate shattered, and the food was left stuck to the gradient countertop.

"You're about to be almost sixty-seven years old and having a baby with a twenty-four-year-old. You've got to be kidding me."

"Lil' girl, you done lost your damn mind! You better respect me in my house. I'm still your father."

"Are you though?"

Ding dong!

The doorbell stopped us from destroying what was left of our fucked-up relationship. Losing two parents in this lifetime was more than the average person could handle. Knowing that both parents might still be alive and not love you was a-whole-nother beast. These were the cards I was dealt. The difference this time around was I loved myself more. My peace was my first priority, and this wasn't it, as much as I wanted it to be. I stormed to the front door with my father on my heels.

I grabbed up my heels and snatched the door open. I stopped in my tracks.

"Monica, what are you doing here?" my father asked his suga baby.

"My mother threw me out," she mumbled. I hadn't noticed the black garbage bags scattered on the front lawn.

"Instead of you worrying about my potential relationship, you need to be worrying about how you are going to put another kid through college." I pushed past Monica, almost wishing she wasn't pregnant so I could drag her.

You would have thought I ran to my car with how quick I got in. I put my car in drive, releasing a new set of tears. You'd think my tear ducts were depleted. I was tired of crying, but I was more tired of not living. What made it even worse, I hoped like hell my father didn't stay mad at me long. When he shut me out for long periods of time, I felt lonely without family to call my own, wondering who would care if I died.

BUSINESS WAS PICKING up for Major Cutz, and that was with no marketing. Word of mouth went a long way when you had great customer service. I didn't want to just open a barbershop; I wanted men to have somewhere to come to relax and relate. Real soon, we would be adding king facials and some other services for a whole experience. We had to stand out if we were going to stay afloat in a saturated market, and Matt, the barber, couldn't agree more.

"I think we have a solid plan." I looked on as Matt gathered up all the papers of our many ideas.

"This is only the beginning of what I know will keep our appointments booked. If we keep it up, these dudes won't want to go home."

We both laughed at Matt's statement, but it was true; we were trying to build a safe space for conversation and therapy for all men.

That was something I never had. My therapy was making people suffer for the things that happened to me that I couldn't control as a kid. I never realized how much my past was in line with what I was trying to accomplish here in the shop. I always needed a safe space to get groomed and to learn something about manhood, but for some reason, that wasn't available to me. Ruby tried her best, but she couldn't teach me how to be a man. Our emotional intelligence had two different definitions. In some way, this was my way of giving back, kind of like what Ruby did for us but with positive resources.

"Yo, I'm about to be out. Lock up. I'll see you tomorrow." I dabbed Matt up, gathered my things, and made my way to my truck.

Every time I walked out the doors of the shop, I looked, hoping to see Mona—always trying to get a glimpse of her smile, beastin' to inhale the sweetness of her scent, and catch sight of what she was wearing. Her beauty was unmatched. Mona was always well put together, but I knew there was more to her than what I saw. That was the interesting part of getting to know someone, and it felt good to finally be able to. Before I could make it to my truck, Mona's Kia flew by almost doing eighty miles per hour. I could spot her car anywhere and speeding into the parking lot wasn't like her. I rerouted my steps in her direction to check her temperature.

Mona bolted toward the art gallery before I was able to get to her. I picked up my pace, always thinking the worst out of habit. I was also checking to make sure nobody was following her just in case I had to use the rounds of my chamber I had tucked away. I made my way inside the gallery in pursuit to meet Mona's need, whatever that was. I made it to her office door; it was cracked, and I watched her release a silent cry as she looked in the full-length mirror. Her hands were over her mouth, trying to hold in whatever life threw her way.

I didn't want to startle her, so I knocked lightly on the door. We locked eyes through the mirror, connecting in a way that built trust for this very moment. Mona didn't wipe her eyes or the snot that came from her outpour. I made my way over to her while we kept our eyes locked on each other. She rested her head on my chest as I encased my arms around her and took a deep breath, which meant it was time for her to release what had made her emotionally vulnerable.

"My father hates me, and no matter how hard I try, I still care," Mona managed to get out.

"The key words are that you care, and that's not a bad thing. It may not seem like that at the moment, but there is a silver lining somewhere in there." I didn't always think like that, but Mona was a true testament that it was true for some.

"I don't know if I believe that. I rather not be the chosen one. I didn't ask for any of this." Mona broke from my embrace to face me.

"Would you like to share what happened?" If she wasn't up to giving me details, that was okay, too.

"What were your parents like?" Mona asked, softly. I wasn't expecting that, but I had to respect the question at hand.

I wasn't the sharing type, but in this very second, Mona needed me to be an open book.

"My mom disappeared when I was about nine, and her blood was on my father's hands. It was never proven, but in my heart, I know he killed her." I took a deep breath, realizing that was a lot for the average person.

"Wow, Mega. Do you keep in contact with your father?" she asked innocently.

"He died in jail, doing a bid for armed robbery. After my mom's disappearance, I never saw him again. 'Til this day, I don't know if they found my mother's body." I never uttered these words to anyone else except A'shai and Mya. Ruby knew what happened, but it wasn't me who told her. There had to be a genuine connection that Mona and I shared. Those words leaving my mouth were still uncomfortable; it was my reality though.

"How did you find out that he died in jail?" Mona grabbed my hand, leading us to the two chairs in front of her desk.

"They had to notify the next of kin, and I was listed. I ripped the letter up and kept doing me. That was the day I knew I had to build my own legacy, write my own story. When it clicked, there was no time to look back on the past. How important is your legacy to you?" With her father's approval or not, Mona had to realize that her greatness lay within.

"My legacy has always been wrapped around my family's name, and my father was the patriarch. Without his blessing, what do I have?" Mona sat facing me. Even in the state she was in, she managed to look heavenly.

"One day, your father will be giving you away to your husband." He would have no choice if I had anything to do with it.

"What if he doesn't want to give me away? I told him about you, and he flipped." Mona's eyes grew weary.

"This is what this is about?" I questioned. I understood fathers were overprotective of their daughters, but Mr. Sutton was taking it a little too far.

"Do my daddy issues scare you?" Mona avoided my question with a question.

"Nothing scares me. What you're going through only shows me your heart and how pure it is. There're only a few people who possess the qualities of a person that will give you the clothes off their back just so the other person can be warm." I bet even if Mona was cold, she was content, knowing she helped someone else. That was how she operated; every day, she put people's feelings and needs before her own.

"Okay, it doesn't scare you, but does it deem me unworthy to be loved?"

I didn't understand what one had to do with the other.

"You, unworthy? Absolutely not. All the love you receive is because you deserved every bit of it. Yes, we both had messed up childhoods, but that was no fault of our own. We literally played the hand we were dealt, no matter the game that was on the table." That was how I viewed it anyway.

"Not having my father's support always highlights my other insecurities. It makes me start thinking of all my fears and all the reasons my life turned out the way it did. When does this part of my life get better? Meaning, I shouldn't have to carry the burden of what my mom did or what my father continues to do. When does it stop?"

I had to let that question marinate for so many reasons. For a long time, I wondered the same thing, until I blocked it from my mind. That would make life perfect, and that didn't exist in a world of chaos. I also didn't want to be the bearer of bad news. Mona was too sweet of a person to have to deal with the reality that life happened. The more I was around her, the more I wanted to shield her when things were thrown her way. I wasn't quite sure if she was ready for that, but I was willing to wait and see. We both had things we were working through in the present, but our future was looking strong.

"I can't promise that you'll ever stop having to carry the load. What I can promise is, if you keep me around, I can help you carry it." I meant every word, understanding life alone was hard, so having a support system was beneficial to a healthier life.

"It's heavy. Are you sure you'll be able to manage?"

I got up from the chair, scooped her up, and sat back down with her in my lap.

"Trust me, that will not be a problem." I kissed the top of her head while she rested her whole body on my chest.

We both sat silently for a few minutes, I guess taking in all that had been shared. When you opened yourself to share, you always wondered if the other person could handle the heaviness. Most people thought that if it was too heavy for them, why burden someone else with the extra weight. It was hard to ask for help, especially when you needed it your whole life and it never manifested. One thing about me, I lent a helping hand when I saw a loyalty to love, morals, and values. This was a lot for one night.

"How about we get some takeout and watch a movie at my house?" Mona got up to stretch, her mood had shifted a little.

"Say no more. My movie picks are just as fire as my music playlist." I was down, but I couldn't stay the night. I didn't know how I would slip away. I'd just deal with that when it was time.

"What movie comes to mind for tonight?"

Mona wanted to see what I would come up with quickly.

"Tonight, let's watch Strictly Business." It was the first movie that came to mind, and it wasn't a bad pick.

"I'm down for that. Let's do P.F. Chang's for takeout. That way we don't have to go far. I'll order it right now."

The way Mona lit up when she talked about food always made me smile, knowing that was her happy place.

We waited the time given for our order to be ready, making small talk about some of our favorite movies and TV shows. Mona didn't want to leave her car, so she tailed me to get our food, and then we jumped on the highway to her house. When we arrived, a Lincoln MKG was parked in the driveway, and someone was on her porch. It was an older gentleman that appeared once I was able to get a clearer view. Mona parked on the other side of the car, and I found a park on the street, grabbing our food.

"Daddy, what are you doing here?" Mona asked once she was able to make it out of her car.

"I came here to apologize for how things were left between us." Her dad looked my way once I made it to Mona's side. "Did you order food? Who's this?"

He knew damn well I wasn't a delivery guy; it was a nice try though.

"No. This is Mega, the guy I was telling you about."

"Yeah, the guy I told you to stay away from."

Her dad raised his voice, making her jump a little.

"Maintain low tones with her." I tried my best not to get involved in family business, but I refused to let Mona live in fear while I was around.

"Was I talking to you… you vagabond?" Dude directed his anger at the wrong person.

"I was talking to you though. Mona is grown and can make her own decisions, and you must trust you raised her right."

"Obviously, I didn't if she has you speaking for her."

Her dad took his eyes off me and spoke to Mona like he was disgusted.

"If you want to throw away your life, do it, but don't expect me to be a part of it. When he leaves you pregnant and broke, don't come running back to me."

His words were like weapons trying to break her down, and I wasn't having it.

"Listen. You're lucky I respect you for being Mona's father. I don't know how long that's going to keep me from whupping your ass." I stepped in front of Mona to block her just in case her father's words turned physical.

"You see, this is the type of men you choose? The cops

would have a field day with you, but you are not even worth me dialing the number."

Her dad stormed off, not saying another word. He slammed his car door, aggressively backed out the driveway, and sped off.

"I'm sorry you had to hear all that."

I turned around, realizing Mona was watching her dad pull away as if he was never coming back. I was hoping one day he would be able to move on from it; from the looks of it, I doubted it.

"Thank you for taking up for me. Nobody ever did. Not too many people got to witness this side of my father. Now all I want to do is get in the bed so I can wake up tomorrow and leave this day in the past. I'm going to take a rain check on our movie night; please don't be mad at me." Mona looked up at me with pleading eyes.

I didn't want to leave her in this state, but I had to respect her wishes. I wanted to hold her all night, but that would only complicate things anyway because I couldn't sleep over. That was a conversation for another day, and right now, I needed to be there for Mona. Giving her space wasn't how I thought the night would end, but that was where we were. I reluctantly gave in, wrapping her in my arms as I kissed her forehead, stepped back, and watched her walk in the house and close the door.

I gotta do something special for her.

With each step to my truck, my thoughts started running wild on how to make her smile.

MONA LISA SUTTON

Truth be told, I was nervous as hell, which I didn't understand. I'd been around Mega a lot these past few weeks. If he wasn't stealing me away for lunch, he was stopping by just to say hi. I didn't even know if he had a girlfriend. It didn't stop me from cumming all over his face, either. He made me nasty and allowed me to let out my inner freak. I'd only given my body to one man before Mega, and it turned him gay. Although Terrell probably knew he was gay way before we hooked up, it still bothered me from time to time. I never knew that a man like Mega existed on this side of earth.

"Girl, where is he taking you tonight? He is all romantic and shit. I likes me a romantic ass dude." Gina gave me her rundown of her idiosyncrasy.

"He said it's a surprise. Girl, and you know how much I hate surprises, but with him, I look forward to them." I closed my eyes as Gina sprayed the setting mist after she was done with my makeup. I looked at myself in the vanity mirror, admiring the woman I was becoming. I was a late bloomer, but I finally could say I was getting the hang of it.

"A bitch knows what she doing, don't she?" Gina caught me checking out her work.

"Yes, friend. Yes!" I had to give props where props were due. She had me looking like a fashion model for the plus-sized women catalogs. I still wasn't completely sold on the shape of my body. I lost a lot of weight, but I thought I could stand to lose a little more.

Mega said he wanted me to wear something relaxed. His words were, "As much as I love to see you in heels, this date doesn't require that." The way his tongue met his pink, lickable lips was what I remembered the most. I wasn't a sneaker girl, so my red and white checkered Vans repped my walk. My light indigo, high-rise ripped jeans and red and white racerback tank top completed my look. What I focused on the most in the mirror before me was the smile I was wearing. That added an extra accessory to the outfit.

"That dick must be good; you glowing. You better not be pregnant." Gina laughed while packing her things to leave.

"Get out my house!"

"Girl, when the dick good like that, you gotta take a pregnancy test every time he gives you some." My stomach was hurting from laughing. Gina was a damn fool.

One thing my girl was right about, Mega was putting it down. At first, I thought it was because I really didn't have anything to compare it to. Nope. The more he talked to me with his strokes, the more it was evident that pussy was his specialty. Those flashbacks would have me weak in the knees during meetings and debriefing with my team. You would think he had the controls to a panty vibrator that was between my legs. At this point, I was going to enjoy riding this wave of euphoria.

"All jokes aside, Mo. I'm happy to see you smile. That new slong is not getting all the credit, either." Gina made a popping sound with her mouth and rolled her eyes. "The fact that you are finally living out your dream is what unlocked the bad bitch you see in the mirror today. Work that shit, sis'. You deserve it."

"If I cry, it's your fault." I fanned my face, giving Gina a hug. I opened the door to let her out.

"Boy, you can't be standing there like that. I'm from the hood. We shoot people for that shit." Gina almost collided with Mega's brick stature and the peach Juliet roses that were centered in his hand.

"My apologies, Kill Bill." His deep baritone caused the hairs to stand up on my body.

"I'll forgive you only if you take real good care of my girl here."

"You don't have to worry about that." Mega handed me the roses and wrapped those arms I loved around me. I melted like butter in a pan from the heat of his body.

"Let me go call your brother." Gina stuck out her tongue and was on her way. We watched her get in her car and pull away.

"I know something is wrong with my friend. You don't

have to tell me." We both let out a hearty laugh. "Come in. I just have to get my purse and put these in some water." I stepped to the side to let him in so I could close the door.

My heart rate sped up for some reason. Mega being in my personal space had to be voodoo because I was falling for him. The European white oak flooring led the way to the kitchen of my townhome. Sometimes it was surreal that this was my place. I lived in my parents' home all of my life, and this was definitely an upgrade. I had gigantic pella windows that were facing a beautiful park. Fort Lee, New Jersey, wasn't too far from the art gallery.

"Your place is dope," Mega said, admiring the enormous chef's kitchen built with modern European cabinets, sleek, thin profile marble-like quartz, and a king-size kitchen sink. It was all courtesy of my dad, who now that I thought about it probably wanted me out of the house to move his new kid in.

"Thank you. I've only been here for a few months. There's still some things I would like to add." I had a long laundry list of things. I wouldn't bore him with the details. "Let me go grab my purse, and I'll be right back."

"Come here." The way Mega said it had my clit jumping. He summoned me between his thick legs as he was seated at the island. I obeyed his command.

"We gotta go. Didn't you say we had to be somewhere at a certain time?" He'd better stop before I loosened his black Gucci belt.

"We will get there when I say we get there. Right now, I want to kiss your lips. Is that alright with you?" I loved how he always asked for permission, knowing damn well I would say yes. If this was a soundtrack to our life, Floetry's "Say Yes" would be playing as he grabbed me up to take my lips on a journey of intense pleasure.

"Go ahead and go get that purse so we can be out." Mega ended the kiss, teasing the hell out of me. I couldn't say a word. He slapped my ass when I turned to walk away. Everything in me was saying forget this date and get right down to what I was sure we both were longing for. We had all night for that, and I wanted to enjoy this nice, beautiful Sunday, so I did what I was asked.

It didn't take us long to get to our destination once we were out of the house. The ride was smooth in his white Range Rover. Liberty State Park in Jersey City, NJ, was where we ended up. The breeze from the April weather set the tone for this outdoor adventure. Mega grabbed my hand as we made our way through people, as the shores of the Hudson River rocked back and forth.

We made it to our own secluded area of the park that I didn't know existed. My mouth dropped at what I saw before me. There was a pickup truck parked with the back latch down. The back was covered with blankets, pillows, and a spread of food. There was even a mini bar set up. As we got closer, I noticed two sets of trees covered with saran wrap. There were cans of what looked to be spray paint. My suspicion was correct when I noticed a guy who had already started painting on one of the sets of trees.

"Itumeleng!" Mega shouted, taking the guy out of his zone.

"Mr. Da-kar!" The guy's African accent was evident in

his speech. They showed love the only way guys knew how to.

"This is my lady friend, Mona Lisa. Mo Love, this is Itumeleng."

I hoped I didn't have to say his name. I would butcher it, I knew it. I shook his hand and waited for the correlation.

"Nice to meet you, Mona Lisa. I'll be your instructor for the next few hours. All the way from Gaborone, Botswana." Itumeleng's broken English could still be understood.

After our introductions and a walk to the mini bar, Itumeleng explained what we were doing. We were to spray paint the saran wrap and create together, while we sipped some liquor and enjoyed each other's company. This was the perfect date. It had all the things I liked: painting, food —sometimes anyway—some good liquor, and this fine specimen whose eyes were on me as I looked around at all he had done for me.

"Why are you doing all this, Mega?" I couldn't help but ask. Itumeleng threw his headphones on as he finished his saran wrap painting.

"I'm honestly trying to figure out the same thing." He paused for a moment to collect his thoughts and continued. "I can't even front like I'm not feeling you." Mega stopped painting his part of the New York skyline that we agreed to paint.

"That's obvious. Why me though? I'm sure you could have any girl you want." I sprayed my section, waiting for an answer.

"I really can't." Mega's mind went somewhere really quick, but he was able to recollect himself just as fast.

"Well, I'm going to tell you this. My heart can't take another heartbreak." I stopped painting to look him dead in his eyes.

I had to be that girl. Mega had to make things clear to me. I wasn't saying he had to propose, but I needed to know what we were doing. Maybe it was because my father's words were still ringing in my head. Either way, I was standing on my vulnerability, hoping it would hold me up. This was getting real for me. I couldn't fight the feeling. Mr. Mega Dakar was becoming a part of my daily thoughts, so I needed to know something.

"Me either. So we both have that in common." Mega took a sip from his red cup of Henny. "I can't tell you that I won't break your heart because I really don't know. My intentions are not to, but life has a way of making the most honorable men recant that statement."

"After dating my high school boyfriend, I told myself I would never give myself to another man. I still carry that hurt with me. A lot of my insecurities stem from that relationship, along with the fact that I wasn't enough for my mother to stay." It was my turn to sip my drink.

"What if that relationship was preparing you for this one?" I pondered Mega's question. I looked over at him as his smooth skin reflected the sunset.

"If it was, why couldn't I have learned another way? I went through years of torment in my mind. I really believed any relationship I had was doomed from the beginning. If my mother didn't want me, why should somebody else?" A cry was brewing. I needed answers to some real life ish.

"Mo Love... Listen, unfortunately, we can't choose our parents. If so, I would have chosen both my parents to be in my life. That wasn't my reality. Remember, your strength and your character was built from that void. My parents not being there gave me superpowers that I wouldn't have known I had." Mega was putting the finishing touches on the saran wrap as I looked on, having way too much to drink.

"Let me find out you the Black Clark Kent." Our laughs made the conversation a little lighter.

As the sun was setting, we were as well. We finished up our painting, which was super dope, and the one that Itumeleng did was breathtaking. We said our goodbyes to him, and we moved on to the next part of our date. There were lights surrounding the pickup truck as we climbed into the back to relax. The music from the portable speaker was now playing Leon Bridges' "River." Mega didn't lie when he said not to sleep on his playlist.

"I got some good news today," I blurted out.

"I could always use some good news." Mega's eyes were low but alluring under the fluorescent lights. The blunt he smoked had him even more laid back. I was feeling nice myself.

"Today I got a call from Michael Weiss, the Metropolitan Museum of Art president and chief executive officer. Picturesque got selected to host the pre-fundraising gala!" My excitement could be seen from the shoulder bounce I was doing.

"No shit! That's huge." Mega's lips congratulated me. That excited me more.

"We'd been planning for this event way before I opened. The proposal we submitted was accepted. Now all we have to do is put everything in motion." I clapped my hands together, anticipating the doors that would open for Picturesque.

"What can I do to help?"

"The shop can be one of the sponsors. I'll make sure you get on the list. That way, our Black businesses can be in a room of billionaire investors." A part of me wanted to tell him he should be my date.

"I got you, Mo Love. If it's going to make you smile, I'm here for it." Mega's hands met the side of my face. He took a minute before he spoke again. "I'm proud of you."

Mega didn't even know how much that meant to me. It was a moment I'd probably cherish for the rest of my life. It was the beginning of people seeing me, happy, building a Black art dynasty. He grabbed my hand, and we made our way off the truck. Snoh Aalegra's smooth melodic voice on "I Want You Around" conveyed my feelings at the moment. If Mega kept it up, he was going to be around for a long time. His chest became my resting place as we danced.

"Do you believe in fairytales?" It felt like the right question for this instant.

"Fairytales are for females. I believe I'm the creator of every feeling and emotion in my story. My story that is life. Yes, created by God, but I choose which story will be written." The lights and music were the backdrop as we created the fairytale that would be this moment.

"Were you always this wise?" We moved in sync with the words we spoke and moved our feet to the cords of the song.

"When you lived the life that I lived, my wisdom comes from abandonment and trauma that I wouldn't wish on any kid. I learned from that and applied the knowledge given by someone who I thought was wise counsel."

"I thought my dad was wise counsel, too, until he didn't have the authority anymore. Had me wondering if every man was like that." My father's ways had me really believing that every man had control issues.

"There is a difference, and I don't think your father understands that difference. You teach, and you live by what you teach, and it will stick. I think it's immature to force someone to think like you. Everyone has their own identity. It sounds like your father needs to find his." Mega spun me around as the grass under my feet moved with me.

"You seem to have it all together while still living on the edge. Always checking your surroundings, on high alert. What's following you that you don't want to bring to the surface? Or should I say who?"

"I think you reading me wrong, Mo Love. I'm a protector at the end of the day. When you with me, that's my job. It's some crazy people out here. The words caught and slippin' are not in my vocabulary. If you going to kick it with me, get used to it." Mega grabbed me tighter around my waist, almost picking me up off the ground as "Taboo" by Sevyn Streeter played.

"Most men are protectors, I get that. It gotta be more to it than that, right? My father was good at protecting, but he lacked the emotional ability to open himself to other women after he found out that hearts don't break even. Are you able to emotionally give a woman more?"

"I only can give what I can give. Emotions are feelings, and most times, feelings can change without notice. Relationships aren't always easy, but when I find a loyalist and a rider, I do what needs to be done. My goal is to live, and if she gives me a reason to, it will be easy to be invested." Mega kissed my forehead as we rocked back and forth.

"You can come back to my place." I looked up, hoping he didn't want the night to end.

"Say no more." Mega kissed me on my forehead once more.

"You can stay over. I may bless you with some breakfast in the morning if you act right." I winked at Mega, knowing he'd like my cooking.

I immediately felt like I said something wrong. Mega released the hold he had around my waist as we were walking back to get our belongings. One thing about Mega, his eyes spoke for him. Was it too soon for me to ask him to stay the night? Did he not like other people's cooking? Whatever it was had him rethinking some things.

"I can't stay over, but we can rock out for a little while." Mega seemed unsure of his answer.

"Everything in me wants to ask you why you can't, but I won't put myself through that. Take me home." I snatched up my things and stormed out of the park to the parking lot. He wasn't too far behind me. I watched him approach the Range on his phone.

He's probably telling his girlfriend he'll be home late.

Mega ended the call before sitting in the driver's seat. He started the car without a word. We rode a few minutes before he opened his mouth.

"I'm still working through some things. It's not what you think—"

"Says every man who has a woman at home waiting on him. What, it's complicated?" Mega never answered my question. He kept his eyes on the road until we pulled up in front of my house. I wasted no time grabbing the handle to exit. He stopped me. I wanted to fight the feeling, but I released my hand from the handle.

"She died in my arms." Mega now had my undivided attention, trying to figure out who he was talking about. "God needed her more." My heart dropped. I rubbed his chest, hoping it would soothe him. I waited for him to finish.

"My fiancée's name was Mya, and she died in her sleep from a brain aneurysm. I haven't slept much since then. If I stay with you, a part of me is scared that you'll never wake up." That broke my heart. This big strong man had real fears that went beyond his outer alpha. "Give me some time. I promise you it'll be worth it." Mega grabbed my hand and kissed it like the first time we'd met.

I was speechless, so I exited the car, not knowing what else to say. I looked back toward the Range but couldn't see inside because of the tint. I hoped he knew he could come in if he needed me. As much as I needed time to process what he told me, I wanted to be there for him. I was sure I wouldn't be getting much sleep tonight.

MEGA DAKAR

"Babe, wake up. If you don't stop playing and get your ass up."

Silence.

"Mya, why do your body feel so cold? You should have told me to turn down the air conditioner." I stood frozen at her side of the bed.

My heart started beating, stifled by the what if. I grabbed her right arm and checked her pulse. The knots in my stomach rumbled, bringing me to my knees. I held her close, praying and hoping that God would hear me. I found the strength to get to my feet. I checked to see if my prayer worked as I brought Mya close to me. It was as if she was sleeping peacefully. Many nights, I watched her sleep, knowing I was a lucky man.

To know she would never wake up again stopped my heart.

I jumped out of my sleep. The sweat that covered my body soaked through my satin sheets. I shifted myself toward the headboard and laid against it. That day still haunted me. That was why my sleep ratio was off. Painting gave me the courage to be relaxed enough to close my eyes, even if it was only for a few hours.

I made my way to the small gym to let off some steam to start my day. The meeting with Gavino was in a few hours. I had ample time to get my mind right for the task at hand. I was also sure thoughts of Mona would cross my mind. The way she smiled when I told a corny joke; the way she got excited and always danced when she ate food, after trying her hardest not to indulge in such a guilty pleasure. It was cute, but it also was a trigger for something way deeper. My hour workout had a packed agenda, and I crushed it. I took a shower afterwards and got dressed. A'shai called right on time.

"What it do, brethren?" A'shai was ready to make those moves.

"I'm ready, A. I'm coming out now, pimpin'." I did a double check, making sure I had all that I needed. Tonight I had Sanction with me, my Glock 19, easy to tuck away, but I also had my Swiss SIG SG 550 assault rifle. That was if Gavino wanted to get stupid. I didn't trust anyone outside of A'shai.

"Took you long enough, nigga. Damn," grumpy ass A'shai let it be known once I made it in the passenger seat of his Jeep Grand Wagoneer.

"Shut up and pass that blunt. You talkin' too much." We

both laughed. That caused A'shai to cough his lungs out after his last pull before he passed it.

"I know we went over this, but let's make sure we are on the same page," I said before taking my first pull. "That last job messed all of us up. Losing one of our own had me rethinking."

"We solid like them shoulders holding that big ass head." A'shai had jokes, causing his laugh to echo through the Jeep. We were done with our shit talkin', so we moved to the business at hand.

"You think Ruby is going to show her face?" A'shai looked at me quickly before putting his eyes back on the road. This sativa hitting my lungs had me feeling invigorated.

"Knowing her, she'll be somewhere lurking. It don't matter; we doing this on our terms. If Gavino don't like that, we will find another way to get you right, A." I was only doing this for him anyway.

"I hope she don't fuck this up for me. Nothing standing in my way of getting this paper, not even the lady who raised us." A'shai's veins on the side of his temple pulsated, he meant every word he spoke.

We finished smoking the blunt as we let the music take us to our destination. We both were lost in our thoughts for many reasons. Some thoughts we had in common, and the others we had to deal with as men. The money we were about to make from this job was about to set us up nicely. The last job we did for Gavino, we all walked away with $187,500 while Ruby took a cut of $250,000. That milli was easy money, especially for Ruby, who didn't do anything. I didn't know all the details of this job, but he'd better be talking my language. We were now premium clientele.

"Buonasera, Mr. Dakar and Mr. Blaze." Gavino Contini walked from the back of Carmine's Italian Restaurant in Times Square to greet us. Gavino was a smooth dude, if he wasn't dishonorable. He used his money and his family legacy to live life on his own terms. I didn't know what his relationship was with Ruby or how they crossed paths. All I knew was we made a lot of money overseeing the gun shipment on that last job. It was the night I asked Mya to marry me. You couldn't tell us we weren't rich. We had plans.

"Do me a solid and address me as A'shai." That was A'shai's nice way of saying it.

"We would appreciate it if you called us by our first names." My eye contact with Gavino solidified he was dealin' with lions who knew what they wanted.

"Would you like anything to drink? We also have some food we can bring out." Gavino snapped his two fingers before we had a chance to utter another word.

"Giorgia, bring them whatever they like." Gavino waved his hands toward us. He opened his suit jacket and pulled out a cigar. His silver chrome lighter blew fire as he pulled, exhaling the smoke. He then released the woody aroma into the air.

The restaurant was closed, so there wasn't much going

on but the business we were about to conduct. For the last job, we only met briefly to go over the plans. Ruby did most of the talking as if she came up with the plan. Talking was her thing, so I always took the back seat when dealing with clients. As long as we got our money and I was able to execute the plan how I saw fit, it kept us all happy.

"We good. Thank you, Giorgia." She was a sexy little thing, but she looked scared, like she was being held hostage.

"Sir, is there anything else you would like?"

"Bring me some Disaronno." Giorgia rushed off to go get him his brown liquor.

"When Ruby told me you guys were on board with this next job, I knew it would get done. As I understand, we're doing things a little differently this time. Ruby will be allowing you to handle the negotiation." Gavino sat back in his chair, crossed his leg, and allowed room for deciphering.

"We are the ones doing the work. It's time for us to start handling our own affairs. Is that cool with you?" I didn't want to leave anything unanswered. Both Gavino and Ruby would know where we stood.

"I'll answer that after I tell you why I need your service." He put his cigar down and sat up and continued. "Next month, the Met Ball is hosting their annual fundraising gala held for the benefit of the Metropolitan Museum of Art's Costume Institute in New York City. And this year, they added a new line up to their schedule." Gavino paused to allow the Disaronno to coat the lining of his throat as it went down.

"Sunday night, they will be showcasing antique paintings that are worth a lot of money. There's one that belongs to me and my family. It's finally out of the vault that it was hidden in, and I want to bring it home."

"Why is this antique painting so important?" It had to be more than about money. Gavino wasn't hurtin' for money. He probably was a billionaire.

"It's a family heirloom. It shouldn't have left my family property. Now that it's been located, I'm not going to go back to Italy without it."

"Where is this event being held?" A'shai spoke up, mapping out details in his head. The focused stare told it all.

"The Picturesque Gallery in Hackensack." A'shai and I locked eyes, thrown off by the information we just received.

You gotta be kidding me. My eyes spoke first.

No fucking way. I heard A'shai's voice in my head.

I didn't know what type of game this was or why this was happening, but this couldn't be life. Yet, it was. I shifted in my seat, trying to buy time to think. I couldn't do this to Mona. I couldn't do this to A'shai, either. He was my priority, and in a way, I felt like Mona was becoming my priority, too. I wanted to see both of them happy and living life. I didn't know what was about to happen, but I knew I had to handle my handle, regardless.

"How much bread you talkin'?" Gavino's answer would determine my next question.

"A million dollars. All of you split it the way you like." Gavino took a pull of his cigar.

"We will need $250,000 upfront, and the rest will come to me once the job is done. Not only am I handling the negotiation, but I'm also handling the finances. Are we clear?" I was going to give Ruby a finder's fee, but that was about it.

"Ruby said you would say that. That's not a problem." Gavino sat up and looked me in my eyes. I didn't like the feeling I was getting.

"We'll be in touch in a few days with a detailed plan. Once the plans are finalized, we expect to see that $250,000 within three business days." With that, both A'shai and I got up.

"It's always a pleasure doing business with you guys." Gavino held out his hand. A handshake in our line of work was a signed contact. We locked hands, made eye contact, and we were on our way. A'shai and I walked back to his truck in silence.

A million dollars split two ways was going to go a long way. A'shai said he needed money to leave the game. Hopefully, this was enough for him to do just that. I had to figure out how to get this money with A'shai and keep Mona protected. There had to be a way to get ahead of this unfortunate circumstance. Knowing the layout of the art gallery was a plus and would work in my favor. I had a lot to think about but not a lot of time to do so. I grabbed the handle to the truck and got in position.

"Ruby only getting $50,000, nothing more." A'shai pulled off, hitting the busy streets of New York.

"You're giving her more than I would have, but I'm

cool with that." I lit another blunt to decompress from our meeting.

Gavino paying a million dollars for a painting was still baffling to me. I guessed when you had plenty of money, you brought things that weren't needed. We were down to two men, so we had to pull this job off by ourselves. It was too close to home. We had to make sure not to shit in our own backyard. There were a few key things and minor details that I already had in mind if we were going to do this right. This was going to be a long night.

"Yo, somebody's following us." I turned to look back to see if I could see what he saw. "It's a black Impala with dark ass tint," A'shai said, speeding up. "It looked like he pulled out the same time we did."

"Oh shit. You right. I see them. Lose this motherfucker." I climbed to the back and grabbed my Swiss SIG SG 550 assault rifle, still keeping my eyes on the vehicle.

A'shai hit a hard right, putting the truck on two tires as he turned the corner. He had skills. We didn't flip over, but we were slowly losing the Impala. Even at 115 miles per hour, we still couldn't shake this fool. A'shai hit a sharp left turn and then a quick right, taking the speed up another notch. My heart was racing, adrenaline pumping, and I was ready for whatever. There was a red light coming up, so A'shai jumped the curb, and everybody got out of the way quickly. We hit a sharp right and got back on the road. I looked out the back window and didn't see the Impala yet. A'shai cut right into a parking garage just in time not to be seen.

A'SHAI BLAZE

CLICK CLACK!

Pop! Pop! Pop!

The sound of bullets was music to my ears. The residue from each pull of the trigger was in the air. It invaded each breath as adrenaline pumped through my veins. The heavy metal fit perfectly in my hand. I cleared the chamber of my gun, ready to shoot another round. The killer in me arose and wouldn't let up until I emptied the clip. Sweat poured from my forehead as I zeroed in on the damage I did. My target wasn't hard to hit; hitting targets was more than aiming. You couldn't teach that. It had to be a part of your DNA.

Until I found out who'd been shooting at and following us, I had to let off steam some way. The gun range was where I spent the last two hours letting the bullets fly. It was a privately owned establishment with limited access to the public, so I wasn't too worried about who was coming in and out. The dope part about it was the attached gym next to it. I didn't have anybody to talk shit with, so I zoned out, lifting pound after pound. Usually, one of my brothers would be with me. We were thick as thieves, really living it out and enjoying the fact that we weren't dead or in jail.

Can't say that now.

Buzz, buzz, buzz

I looked down at the phone after placing the 250 pounds back on the bar. I felt it vibrating at the edge of the bench. The screen lit up with Gina's name that had emojis added. I chuckled because emojis were not my thing, and she was the only contact that had them. When I had her add her number to my phone, I didn't even double check to see how she locked it in. That was before we got our next work order.

She can be my stress reliever.

"What type of games you playing? I been gave you my number." Gina's loud but sexy voice came through my phone.

I had to rethink her being my stress reliever.

"When you call my phone, you acknowledge me and throw in a good morning just for the hell of it." I see she was going to be a hard one to tame.

"Boy, whatever. I don't know what you think this is." Gina's laugh gave me no choice but to laugh along with her.

"I'm not really a phone person. If we gon' talk, let's meet up and do that." I hated talking on the phone. That never was my thing.

"So you just want me to rearrange my schedule for you? There you go again thinking you can tell me what to do." The sass in her undertone made my dick jump.

"I want to see if you have all that mouth when I see you later. Whether you agree to it now or agree to it later. Tonight at nine p.m. I'll shoot you the location." I wanted to get back to my workout.

Silence invaded the two-way call.

"Play with a bitch like me and watch me show you," Gina finally worked up the nerve to say. It was believable to her, but I saw right through it. Her panties were wet.

"Show me tonight. Enjoy the rest of your day thinking about me. Don't worry; it will be here before you know it. Peace." I hung up the phone, shaking my head. I doubt if she knew what she had just gotten herself into.

For the first time in a long time, as a grown man, I felt displaced. Money couldn't solve the thoughts of being alone on a cold kitchen floor, hungry, fighting my body to go to sleep. I couldn't because my stomach was making loud noises. That was where Mega found me when we were youngins after I disappeared for a few days. That day, we vowed to stick together. Life moved so fast after that I never had a chance to look back. We met Ruby not too long after and formed a brotherhood with Star and Tone.

I had this nagging feeling ever since the other night that I just couldn't shake. I wasn't sure if it was because we were being followed and Mega was being shot at, or I felt like Mega was about to switch up on me. The latter was a feeling I never had, but death by association had a way of formulating thoughts that shouldn't be. It had always been money over everything else, but a shot of love would change that, too. This job was already complicated. We were two men down, and now with an extra layer added, it became that much more difficult. I finished up in the gym and took my ass home to take a shower. I had to get ready for our planning session.

"Oh shit, you brought out the detective board." I had made it to Mega's crib, ready to go over these plans. I had a few things in mind. Hopefully we were on the same page.

"You know I'm a visual person." Mega pulled out the big dry erase board, like the detectives on TV shows.

"You got a lot of shit up there. So this means we *are* doing the job?" It was a question I'd been itching to ask him ever since our meeting with Gavino.

"I always keep my word; I told you I was going to do it, and I meant that." Mega looked at me with reassurance that we ride together and die together.

There were different forms of death. In this case, it could be the death of Mega and Mona's situationship. I knew he had to have that on his mind. The way he looked at Mona, I could tell he was feeling her. I never wanted him to feel like he had to choose; unfortunately, when duty called, it had to be answered. The phone number would soon be disconnected once this job was finished. Slowly but surely, I was coming to terms with that. That was another weight I had to carry, but these muscles could lift anything.

"What you going to do about Mona?" That was the million dollar question.

Mega was silent for a minute, collecting and calculating his thoughts. I knew him all too well.

"Let me worry about that. I have something in mind."

We all had a part to play on our team of hard knocks. We played our parts really well until there wasn't a team to play with. Mega was always the captain, the one running the plays on the field, and this time, it was no different, so I wasn't sure of the uneasiness that came with his answer. I put the brakes on those thoughts, just to see how everything would play out. We had a little over a month to watch it all unfold before us.

"Tone is still out there lurking. I put a bolo out on him, but he's been ghost. If we are being followed, how would that work with what we're trying to do?" That was a question that had been rolling around my head since the speed chase with the Impala.

"He's no match for us. I taught him everything he knows. He'll show his face sooner or later. We'll be ready for him." Mega's eyes grew darker as his killer gaze gave me something to look forward to. I had already made up my mind. The next time I saw Tone, I wasn't giving him a pass off the strength of Ruby anymore. We were where we were because of him.

Bitch ass nigga.

"I like how you talkin', bro'." The opposition never stopped us before, so they wouldn't stop us now. We had the blueprint. Pussies like Tone were carbon copies of real-life loyalists. We put the G in gangsta shit.

"I'm going to be there already as a guest. I'll let you in the back door. You've been in the back but probably never paid it any attention, but I created a map for you." Mega pointed to the map he created on the dry erase board.

"What about the security cameras?" I peeped them all around the gallery the first time I was there without even looking for them.

"I know where the hard wiring is. I'll disable it before letting you in." Mega brought my attention to where the security wiring was on the map.

"Did Gavino send you the pictures of the painting as a reference?" I couldn't take something if I didn't know what it looked like.

Mega grabbed a manila envelope that housed the pictures of the painting. He handed them to me, and I looked at every detail. Whoever painted this didn't have anything on Mega and his skills. I couldn't believe that it was worth the money we were getting for it. I didn't see the hype, but that wasn't what I was hired to do. I was pretty sure Mega worked out all the kinks for the part he would play in this operation. Now all I had to do was think through the movement of my steps.

I knew just who to talk to, to make my job just a little bit easier.

Gina with the emojis.

MONA LISA SUTTON

DING DONG.

I wasn't expecting company, and not too many people knew where I lived, so I wondered who it could be. My heart started pounding, thinking it was Mega. I was hoping like hell that it was him. The more I was around him, the more I longed for the laughs and the good conversation. Who was I fooling? The way he made me cum was numero uno in the thought department. Everything else was a bonus. My feet sped up, ready to get to the door to look him over. Gina would have texted or called me, and plus we were going out later, so it had to be him.

"Who is it?" I put on my sweet and sultry voice.

"Baby girl, it's your dad." I rolled my eyes, not up for his shenanigans.

I slowly opened the door, hoping that I would get the person who loved me unconditionally, the one who wore a cape for life's bumps and bruises, the man I wanted to walk me down the aisle.

I was met with roses and a big smile that told me God answered my prayers. This was a surprise to me, and I couldn't be happier. I'd been so engrossed in my work that I hadn't had time to even give me and my dad's disagreement any thought. Mega was a big part of that as well. Life no longer stopped for my dad's feelings. I had goals to meet and life to enjoy, and I did everything in my power to keep reminding myself of that.

"Hey, Daddy. What are you doing here?" I was checking his temperature. What you saw was not always what you got.

"I wanted to come by and apologize for how I acted." He handed me the roses and leaned in for a kiss.

"You really hurt my feelings, Daddy." I moved from the doorway to let him in the house.

"I know, baby girl, and I was out of line for how I spoke to you." He made his way in the house, continuing his apology. "There's a lot of things you don't know that I couldn't bring myself to tell you. I was ashamed, thinking I was a weak man."

"Whose fault is that?" I laid the flowers down on the coffee table in my living room where we now were seated.

"It's nobody's fault but my own. I thought I was protecting you." My dad shifted in his seat.

"Nope. All I got was childhood trauma that cost me a lot of sleepless nights, a lot of tears, and a whole lot of heartbreak." I never was truly honest with my dad because his feelings were already hurt from the time my mother left.

If holding back tears was a person, my dad would be the prime example in this moment. I never saw my father cry before, not even when my mother packed up and hauled ass. He knew how to turn his emotions on and off. When I got my degree and started working as a teacher, he screamed it from the rooftop how proud he was of me. I also saw how cold and standoffish he could be when I finally wanted to start following my dreams. His love came with expectations, and it wasn't healthy for me or him.

"You know, you remind me so much of Geneva that sometimes I have to do a double take to make sure she didn't come back." I couldn't believe he said my mother's name. Usually, when referring to her, it was always my mother or a derogatory term that described her.

"How would I know; you took all the memories I had of her away." I only had a picture that I stole from the attic when I was a little girl.

"I was hurt, baby girl, and I still am. I never loved anyone the way that I loved your mother. She gave me purpose and some of the best years of my life. She gave me you." My dad's right hand met his heart as a sentimental gesture of love.

"Life is what you make it, and being grumpy and mean to your daughter is not the life that I needed." I paused for a quick minute. "You know how many nights I needed you… or even now, how much I need you to say that you are proud of me?" Now, tears were gathering at the brim of my eyelids.

"Most girls had their mothers, but you didn't, and look at you. I will always be proud of how strong and beautiful you are. You beat the odds. You showed the world that life didn't stop. I always wondered how you bounced back so quickly, but then I realized you probably turned it off to cater to me and keep peace in the house."

"Yeah, you are proud of my traits and beauty, but what about my accomplishments?" I looked at him, tears now breaking free.

"Stop looking for validation from people about your work." Once it came out, he regretted saying it. It was written all over his red face.

"People! People! I don't care about people! Their opinions don't matter, and what I'm learning the hard way is that sooner than later, yours won't matter either." I wiped tears from my eyes, wearing my frustration on my sleeve.

"What I meant is, your mother wanted the world to see how talented she was. She did everything to get the attention of the powers that be. She worked day in and day out on her craft, so much so she quit her job to do so." My dad's blood started to boil as he talked about the one he let get away. I never had any solid proof that he fought for her and their relationship.

"I don't see anything wrong with that."

"Of course you don't, baby girl. You are your mother's child. You have the same sparkle in your eyes that she had when the brush touches a blank canvas. All these years, I tried to dim that light." My dad put his head down, owning up to his mistakes.

"You dimmed it, but it never went out," I said proudly.

My dad's blank stare took him somewhere for a minute. This was the most my dad ever talked about my mom.

All I would get was little pieces to a puzzle that was my existence. Once upon a time, not too long ago, my dad and my mom were in love, and I was the product of that. I always wondered if my mom ever wanted to take me with her, or if she came back after missing me. As a woman, I didn't think I'd ever leave my kid to wander around this crazy world aimlessly. It would have made life much easier, I kept telling myself. Who knew if that would have been the case. That has always been my dream reality.

"Your mother had skills. When people witnessed her artistry, they marveled at the way each painting captured the very essence of the matter." A smile spread across my dad's face, reliving that moment of discovery. He continued.

"No matter how talented she was, it was hard to break into the industry. It was male dominated and wasn't looking to add a woman to the fold. Once she quit her job, we started to struggle. I was a college graduate making pennies as a teacher. She booked amateur art showcases but they were few and far between. I no longer saw the love in her eyes. After a while, she started staying out late, and her whole group of friends started to change." My dad shook his head as he flipped through his prefrontal cortex.

"Why couldn't we just move with her? To wherever she went?" Was that a sacrifice he wasn't willing to make for me? He should have known I needed my mother.

"I never got a chance to, baby girl. Your mom got accepted into a program to study abroad and never looked back. Your mother fell in love with somebody else and never gave me a chance to fight for our love. She made promises that she never kept, all for the love of art." My dad balled up his fist, hitting it on the palm of his other hand.

"You never talked to her after she left?" It was like I was watching it all unfold in front of me. I was lost in the details. What a time to be alive to witness the story of Mr. Kurt Sutton and Ms. Geneva Sutton.

"She would send postcards in the beginning, but once I received those divorce papers, I knew she wasn't coming back. A whole year of waiting, hoping she would return once her immersive international experience was out of her system. That never happened, and I was left to pick up the pieces." My dad was finally able to look me in my eyes. The man in him wouldn't let him cry, but it broke my heart to see him turn into that young man again.

"Daddy, I really do appreciate all that you have done for me." I got up to join him on the sofa he was on. "If you would have told me this, I would have understood you a little more." I laid my head on his shoulder.

"Not dealing with it was easier, baby girl." He wrapped his arms around me.

"You didn't deal with it then, so you have to deal with it now. It's time you go to therapy." I pulled back to look him in his eyes. I was serious; I planned to go myself.

"Maybe it is time."

My heart smiled.

"You don't know how much I needed this drink, girl," I said between sips of my apple martini.

"I can tell. You are on your second one, you lush." Gina had a lot of nerve as she slurped up her strawberry margarita.

"I read some of my diary about my life today, parts I didn't even know existed." The conversation with my father was at the top of my brain.

"Nobody don't want to read about your boring life… You know what, now that I think about it, I would love to read about the nasty adventures that Mr. Mega's pipe takes you on."

"You are so nasty." I playfully hit Gina on her arm. "I'm serious though. My dad put a lot of shit in perspective."

"Was it the closure you needed?" For once, my friend got serious.

"I don't think I'll ever get closure. My mom is the only one that can give that. My heart to heart with my father tonight proved to me that you have to do what makes you happy. My dad's anger was rooted in a garden of past transgressions. The wrong seeds were being watered after the storm, and my dad didn't have it in him to plant again."

"That's some deep shit, Ms. Iylana Vanzant Junior." Gina had too many drinks. We cracked up laughing.

"You really get on my nerves."

"Girl, you love it. Did your dad tell you what he was going to name your sister or brother?" I almost spit out my drink at Gina's question.

"One thing at a time. We haven't gotten that far. Damn,

why did you have to remind me of that?" I rolled my eyes. It was my reality either way, so I had to embrace it sooner or later.

"Please forgive me, massa." Gina's dumb self was shaking like she was afraid.

One thing about Gina, she was going to make a joke, bringing light to a dark situation. That was what I appreciated about her. She let me get my thoughts and feelings out, allowing me to hear myself as a way to help sort them out. We'd been rocking with each other for a minute now, so we knew each other like the right Twix knew the left. We experienced many life lessons together, and I couldn't have asked for a better friend. A crazy friend, nonetheless, a friend indeed.

"Mona, is that you?" Both myself and Gina looked to the front of the restaurant, trying to put a face to the flamboyant voice asking the question. "That is you, oh my God. How are you doing?" Terrell came sashaying his ass over to our table with a few queens following behind him.

"Oh shit. His lace front is giving, honey," Gina whispered before Terrell had a chance to make his way before us.

My heart was pounding like crazy, and my hands immediately got sweaty. My breathing slowed up, making it almost impossible for me to breathe in the right amount of air to keep me alive. This was my first time seeing Terrell since his parents sent him away after he came out. His father blew a head gasket when he found out and shipped him to military school. By the looks of it, it didn't work. He had his nails done, hair done, everything did.

"You look good, Ms. Mona Lisa." Terrell snapped his fingers in the air three times. Those same acrylic fingernails used to rub between my legs. I almost threw up in my mouth.

"Thank you. So do you," was all I could say, still in shock that this was actually happening.

"I never got a chance to apologize for you know... I should have been real with you from the jump." He reached for my hand, and I jumped, not anticipating his touch.

"Uh, you jumping like she got cooties or something," the ugliest queen of them all had the nerve to let out his mouth.

"Bitch, don't try it!" Gina shot the ugly duckling a mean mug.

"Who you callin' a bitch?"

"Bitch, you not Queen Latifah and this ain't female empowerment, so miss me with the garbage." Gina rolled her neck in the motion of, I wish a bitch would.

"Peaches, y'all go to the car. I'm coming," Terrell told his entourage before wigs started flying. Peaches snatched the keys and stormed out the restaurant with the other two on his heels, leaving Terrell, me, and Gina.

"What's done is done. That was years ago. There's no need to bring it up." Clearly, it was something that he'd been wanting to get off his chest.

"You didn't deserve the embarrassment I put you through, and I hope one day you will be able to fully forgive me. Not for me, but for you. Any guy would be lucky to have you as his forever partner." Terrell paused. "Thanks for giving me some of the best years of my life.

Goodnight." With that, he walked away, not leaving any crumbs.

I guessed tonight was the night of closure and understanding. First my dad, and then Terrell. They were two important men in my life. Not Terrell anymore, but he played a major role in my teenage years, ultimately helping shape the woman that I would become. I did feel a little lighter after Terrell's apology, but it still felt weird seeing him all dolled up. It was time for me to move past that part of my life and look forward to the future.

MEGA DAKAR

MONEY WAS EVERYWHERE, as I slowly gathered the wrapped bills, putting them back in the duffel bag. The last time I was making my way to my trunk, I got shot at, but today, I had my shooter with me, so I wished a nigga would. A'shai and I were in front of Ruby's house, stuffing her money back in the bag. I neglected to fully zip it up, so it was spread all over my trunk. We stayed on high alert, not sure when the next ambush would take place. The night hovered over us as the streetlights assisted us in gathering all of Ruby's belongings.

"I think I know what I want to do when this is all over," A'shai spoke, breaking my concentration and thoughts of meeting with Ruby.

"Word, what is that?" I was happy that he was thinking 'bout it instead of waiting until shit hit the fan.

"Real estate is where it's at. I get to make major dough and still work for myself," A'shai said proudly.

"I can see you doing that, bro'." It was a proud moment for sure.

"I've been really thinking about it. I even looked up some programs." A'shai was putting in the work.

"After this job, we will both be ending another chapter and starting a new one. I've been ready, and now it looks like you are, too." I finally zipped the duffel bag up, and we made our way to Ruby's.

We received our deposit from Gavino, courtesy of his driver, and we stayed up all night counting it. We decided to give Ruby her cut now so once the job was done, we didn't have to worry about her. The $50,000 I held in my hands was more than enough, and that $200,000 A'shai and I had split wasn't looking too shabby, either. It was definitely more where that came from. We had $750,000 more to collect upon completion.

Ding dong.

Ruby's loud doorbell signaled her that she had visitors.

"Hey, boys." Ruby opened the door for us with a greeting of open arms. Her embrace was always welcomed growing up since we never really got it from our parents. Times had changed, so the duffel bag replaced where our bodies would be. We walked past her after walking through the door, both of us not saying a word. I didn't know what she thought this was.

"I'm grown. I'm not a boy anymore," A'shai spat. I told this dude to be on his best behavior, and he was starting already.

The sinister smile that was plastered on Ruby's face turned into a scowl in under two seconds. "Who are you talking to?" Her voice even changed from sweet to a menacing undertone. "Your mouth has always gotten you in trouble. Don't let it be that way tonight."

"What you going to do, get the belt? Or better yet, get your son to fight me?" Heat could be felt coming from A'shai's body. He wanted to get his hands on Tone so bad.

"My bullets work, just like his does." Ruby's cat eye frames shot draggers A'shai's way.

"Wait, hold up. You know threats are something we don't take lightly. I don't even know why we doing this with you anyway." The pit of my stomach was trying to tell me something. We had now made it inside her living room. A part of me didn't even want to sit down.

"Money is why you doing it. It's been the same way since the moment I took both of y'all in." Ruby sat down, crossed her legs, and looked through us as we stood. "You're also doing it because you don't have a choice; you already agreed to it."

"Bullshit." A'shai quickly let it be known.

"We believed that at one point, but we got put up on game." It may have taken us a while, but now we saw it for what it was.

"Is that so…" Ruby's black nails met the side of her temple like she was thinking.

"I don't know what games you are playing, but we came to drop off the money to you. We were going to go over the plans with you, but it's not necessary." Ruby wasn't lifting a finger; it was no need.

"I see. First, you kept me out of the negotiations, and now you are keeping me out of the most important part." Her stare spoke words that she wouldn't dare say. Ruby was nodding her head up and down, making a face I couldn't quite understand. That, or I really didn't care.

"Take that $50,000 and call it a day. It's easy money." We didn't need the babysitter making life decisions about a life she was no longer a part of. She was fired the moment she allowed Tone to live another day.

"I'm as much a part of this job as you two are. Until you understand that, you'll be fooled by the power you think you have." I wasn't sure what that meant or if Ruby was going crazy.

"You need to take your own advice." A'shai let it be known. He walked away, shaking his head.

"Have a nice life, Ruby. We've made a lot of money together over the years. That's our thanks for keeping a roof over our heads. I wish this could have ended differently." I left her with final words. We owed her nothing.

Ruby didn't have to see me out. I already knew where the door was. It was bittersweet leaving behind the woman who helped me become a man. We were supposed to rock out until the casket dropped. For Star, it dropped too early. Tone's punk ass had a casket with his name on it. A'shai met me in the front with a blunt dangling from his lips. I couldn't wait for him to pass it. We both climbed in my blacked-out Audi R8 in the still of the night, keeping watch as the tires met the pavement.

It wasn't too late to take Mona to the underground modern speakeasy that I knew she would dig. To the naked eye, the average person wouldn't even know it existed. Membership came with a keycard and premium access to the best wine, liquor, and music money could buy. As soon as we walked through the door, we were greeted with a glass of Bartenura Moscato for the lady, and I had my glass of Hennessy with a large ice cube. I raised my glass, and Mona followed suit.

"Tonight, we celebrate you, Mo Love. You are doing your thing, following your dreams, and looking good doing it."

"When is it going to be my turn to spoil you?" I met Mona's gaze, trying to find the answer in her eyes.

"Mr. and Mrs. Dakar, you can follow me." Mona's eyes grew big at the label that was put on us. I thought it was funny. It definitely wasn't planned.

"So you're not going to correct him?" Mona whispered, holding me around my arm as she looked up at me as we made our way to our private booth.

"I don't have to explain things that don't need explaining. It's none of his business unless you trying to holla at him or something." My pearly whites shone under the dark lighting of the underground, enjoying the beauty that was looking back at me.

You tend to appreciate things more when there's a chance of losing it. My heart sank at the thought of having to take from someone who had accomplished so much. It was a position I didn't like being in. It came along with the business, I guessed. Mona asked me not to break her heart, and by the looks of it, I was going to do just that. I was about to enjoy every moment with her, not knowing if I'd ever get the chance to after next month. We got settled comfortably before resuming our dialogue.

"You never answered my question?"

"What question?" I was playing stupid to hear her say it again. I loved the way it rolled off her lips.

"You know what, I don't even need an answer. I know how to take care of a man." Mona winked, sipping her second glass of wine.

"Oh, really? Don't write a check that your ass can't cash. I'll lay you right on this table and eat you for dinner." She already knew about my tongue game, and if she kept it up, everybody in this establishment would know, too.

"You are so nasty. I was talking about spoiling you."

"I gave you the blueprint; all you gotta do is open up." I licked my lips, ready to slurp up every drop of her juices.

"Listen here, you better stop." Mona twitched in her seat.

"Mr. Dakar, would you like another drink?" The waiter cock blocked.

"I'm good. Thank you, Tony." He looked toward Mona, and she held up her hand, signaling she was good.

"I had a heart to heart with my dad the other night that brought a lot of things into perspective for me," Mona blurted out. I listened intently. "Now I understand more about my pain storage."

"Pain shouldn't be something that you store up. It's the

happy moments that should take up that space." My advice came from experience.

"There was so much pain, so I had to put it somewhere."

"Put it in the toilet with the rest of the shit being deposited into the wasteland. You wasted enough of your years."

"Why you think I'm here with you?" Mona challenged. I found it amusing and sexy.

"You're using me for expensive dates?" We both laughed, knowing that wasn't the truth, but we were enjoying each other's company.

Between the blunts I smoked before picking Mona up and the two large shots of Henny I was drinking, I was feeling nice. These past two days really had me at war in my mind on what to do about this next job. We had a plan that I knew was solid, but the more I spent time with Mona, the more she started pulling back the layers of my existence, making me want to live this peaceful life without any illegal activity.

"Have you been working on your painting?" Mona asked excitedly.

"What painting?" I was completely lost.

"Uh, the painting that we are supposed to be working on to showcase in the art gallery?" Mona's excitement was no more. I completely forgot about that with all the things going on. I could still hold up my end of the bargain.

"Oh, no. I haven't started working on it yet, but I got this. It'll be ready… Wait, when did we say it needs to be finished?" I laughed. We laughed together at my forgetful mind.

"So, Gina talked me into asking you what do you think of showcasing both of our paintings at the pre-fundraising gala for the Metropolitan Museum of Art." Mona playfully put both her hands over her face, hiding from my answer.

"What I tell you? Anything to make you smile, I'm here for it." Mona's eyes lit up with pleasurable admiration.

Oh shit, I got it.

I finally knew how we would pull off this next job to keep everybody happy.

"Let me make a call real quick. I'll be right back," I said to Mona, kissing her forehead and pulling out my phone, heading in the direction of the bathroom.

Ring, ring.

"You good?" A'shai answered.

"Change of plans. I'll fill you in tomorrow," I said confidently.

I made my way back to the table after changing the master plan. Mona was grooving to the music, which seemed to have gotten louder. I could tell she was a little tipsy by her glassy pupils. She wasn't driving tonight, so she could freely enjoy herself with whatever she liked. I sat next to her instead of across from her so we didn't have to yell over the music.

"What gets you access to a place like this?" Mona asked while still moving to the beat of the music.

"Money," I replied. If you had big time bank, you had a way in. "Wealth gives you a buy-in to almost any place, and I learned that at a young age. That's why I think I'm successful. I saw firsthand what people would do for cash."

"Money can't buy you happiness though." Mona's low eyes looked my way.

"It may not buy happiness, but it makes you feel good knowing you can buy anything you want. I believe someone broke came up with that saying." Mona chuckled at my candidness.

"Is getting money your only motivation in life?" Mona's question was genuine as it flowed from her drunken disposition.

"At one point it was, and that's only because of my childhood experience. Before my mother disappeared, there was never food on my table, and I constantly got picked on because of my clothes. That gave me a longing to want more, and I didn't know how I was going to accomplish it until I met my foster mom." I didn't want to bring Ruby up, because I knew Mona would have questions, but Ruby was a big part of my life until, of course, recently.

"That was nice of her to take you in. What's her name? I would like to meet her one day if she is still alive."

Mona said the last part knowing I lost so many people.

"Ruby Rose opened her doors to us; she fed us and taught us a lot about survival. My young mind welcomed all the wisdom she shared, and I started to realize who I really was. Our relationship is a little complicated now that I'm an adult, making my own decisions, so I don't know if you'll ever get to meet her at this point." It was time for me to move on from that part of my life anyway.

"It sounds to me like these adults don't want their kids

to grow up. It's like both Ruby and my dad want to control us like we are puppets. I would never do that to my children."

A seriousness took over Mona as she reflected on her future.

"Every parent who didn't like how they were brought up says the same thing. I'm sure being a parent is no walk in the park. The goal is to offer our offspring a better life than we had; unfortunately, they are still going to have their own perception of what life is like. There is no perfect parent, no matter how hard we try." Kids were never a topic for discussion in our house. We didn't want to bring another kid into this world because of the lifestyle we lived. Our families would be targets, and that was an easy way to bring the toughest person to their knees.

"Do you want kids?"

Mona was asking something I really didn't have an answer to. I heard the way she talked about kids and the passion behind her words, but I wasn't sure if that was something I wanted.

"Good question. When I find out the answer, I'll let you know." If I was going to continue to pursue something with Mona, I knew this subject would come up again.

"Well, I want kids. Here's the thing, though; sometimes I feel like I only want kids to do better than my parents did me. Is that wrong?"

"I wouldn't say it's wrong. I think you are setting expectations that are sure to drain your energy. You'll constantly be in a rat race to prove yourself, and you'll forget the importance of being a parent."

Parenthood wasn't for everybody, especially the weak. You were responsible for a human, someone who would not only be shaped by what you said but by your actions. Your child should be your main focus, and that was a lot of responsibility. I didn't know if I'd ever be a father, but it was something I wouldn't take lightly if ever chosen. As I shuffled through my thoughts, I noticed Mona was in a daze. I wasn't sure what she was thinking about.

"What's on your mind?" I pulled her in closer.

"Wondering where you've been all my life. I'm waiting for someone to jump out to tell me this is all a joke." Mona let out a nervous laugh.

That was the liquor talking some real shit.

"It's easy to feel those feelings; that's a fortification that needs consistency. Open your mind to the possibility that this is our reality. It's the right now; tomorrow doesn't matter, and I really don't care about the days that follow. It's me and you in this breath currently, so let's rock out." I was speaking nothing but facts, even knowing that our days may be numbered.

"That's the thing. To me, that gives the person an out to just leave when tomorrow comes. If you ain't rocking with me for life, I don't want it."

Mona's eyes stayed on me as she lifted her wine glass, drinking it until there was no more.

It was a dangerous game to be lost in the cycle, holding someone to a standard they may not be able to uphold. Even if they agreed in the beginning, that didn't guarantee they would stick around. Mona's response was from the shaping of her whole existence, and that was hard to unlearn. How could someone forget the traumatic experiences that they never asked for? I was able to live with mine, but not too many people could say the same. There were a few lessons that I could teach Mona but in due time with my actions, not my words.

"You know that everybody you meet is not meant for a lifetime? I know you saw them Madea plays." That made both of us laugh.

"That's why I don't make new friends or let new people into my life. It's also why I have conversations like this to get an understanding of all intentions."

Mona sounded like she was mature enough to know exactly what she wanted at this point of her life.

"Would that type of thinking get in the way of us getting to know each other?" Our interactions were not new. We'd known one another for a few weeks now.

"Something is telling me to give you a chance, but my journey to this point is telling me not to." Mona's honesty kind of sobered her up a little.

"I got you. It's not easy to trust someone you've just met. Every second we are together is a step closer to the endless possibilities of a love that may abound." Once the words left my mouth, I realized that we might not get to experience that part of our journey.

"I'm glad you get it, but whatever you do, don't make me regret going against the rules I set in place to protect my delicate heart."

Mona laid her hand on her beating heart to drive her point home to make it a real request.

It was never in the plans to enter this next phase of my

life in this predicament. I mastered the streets and what it took to stay alive; that was easy. This part of life though, didn't come natural to me, but what I learned was a good woman could bring it out. With this next job leaving a question mark with Mona, it was making it a little more stressful than it should be. It was time for me to leave the contract-for-hire business. The liability wasn't worth all that came with the job. My past was standing in the way of my possible future, and it wasn't sitting well with me.

GINA THOMPSON

Face down, ass up, that's the way most men like to fuck, and if he ain't giving it to you, he's giving it to someone else.
—Gina T.

I NEVER SAID I was a licensed counselor or therapist. My site *Girl, Don't Trip* would say otherwise based on my comment section. I had to give them the true facts, no chaser. The question I received from Danielle M. from Memphis was that her boyfriend of two years wasn't knocking her back out like he used to. I didn't know if the dude was cheating, but something wasn't right in the water. Once I gave advice, I never followed up on the outcome. I left everyone room to figure it out. The relationship section of my site always got the most views and love from women all around the world.

I closed my laptop, hyped about my night with A'shai. It'd been a few weeks since I had a night out on the town with some eye candy. His dark chocolate skin and muscles that showed his protruding veins was just enough to satisfy my sweet tooth. I wanted to get chocolate wasted in his magnetism. We never got a chance to go out last week, so I was intrigued by where tonight would lead us. I shot A'shai a text.

I'm ready when you are Mr. Chocolate Bar.

If you stayed ready, you didn't have to get ready. So I was always ready with my face beat to the gods, and the threads that created my outfit were always runway certified.

You keep it up, I'll show you what's inside of this chocolate bar.

A'shai replied under my blue bubble.

I'm allergic to nuts.

I inserted the X-shaped eyes sneezing or blowing its nose into a white tissue emoji and hit send.

Mines organic with a lot of minerals that will clear up your skin, grow your hair, and do your body good. Be outside, I'm almost to you, A'shai replied.

There he went, telling me what to do.

You know what happened the last time you called yourself telling me what to do.

I capped it off with a winking eye emoji.

Don't worry WE gonna handle that.

He sent an eggplant emoji, putting an emphasis on the

we. I didn't think he even knew where his emoji keyboard was. I had a way of bringing people out of their comfort zone. Most men were intimidated by me. A'shai was a different breed from what I could tell. I hoped he knew that I was, too. I wasn't your average chick. I did whatever I wanted, when I wanted, and anyone who had a problem with that could kick rocks. That was why even the good dudes never stayed around too long. If you let my mother tell it, I was damaged goods, anyway.

I heard A'shai pull up. It had to be him with J. Cole blasting through his speakers.

Hope of a better way to cope with the pain
And the scars, than the lean and the coke
And I swear in that moment I wish we were still close.

J. Cole was my boyfriend with his sexy ass. Ever since I saw him perform at my college campus, he'd been babe. He was a storyteller, which was why I had front row tickets to his Forest Hills Drive tour. A'shai and I would get along just fine. Not that I doubted it, but it made me look forward to our night. I gathered my things and made my way downstairs to A'shai's dark blue Jeep Grand Cherokee SRT Sport. It was a really nice truck.

"You can't be blasting music around here like that. What you think this is, the projects?" I melted in his cream interior, looking his way like he'd lost his mind. I didn't care if this was Paterson, this was the good part.

"I do what I want. If you don't know that by now, you'll learn." His face was blank of any wrongdoing.

"Pull off before my neighbor calls the cops. I gotta live around here." I looked him up and down. A'shai only pulled off after he turned the music up. It shook the pavement as we drove away, and I quickly turned it down.

I playfully hit him on his arm, feeling his toned biceps, causing me to look him up and down once more. A'shai's left arm was the driver, and he leaned back cruising the street like he was Usher with a gangsta attitude. His goatee went well with the rich, dark chocolate color of his skin. I smelled weed, but his cologne was still stronger. It was a fresh and adventurous man fragrance. I definitely liked what I saw; I could tell you that much. I wouldn't tell him that though.

"What you looking at?" A'shai caught me staring. The smirk on his face proved my point.

"Boy, whatever. Where are we going?" We jumped on Route 80 going toward Woodland Park.

"If you don't sit back and relax. As a matter of fact, spark this." He handed me a blunt. Ganja got me through plenty of nights in my college days, and it'd been a minute, so I took him up on his offer.

"How you knew I smoked?"

"I didn't. Either you gonna spark it or you want me to play Inspector Gadget. Pick a struggle."

"I guess you need it more than me. Let me hurry up and get you your medicine." I lit the blunt and slowly took a pull to see if I still had it.

We pulled up to Garret Mountain Reservation. It was the next town over from Paterson. I guessed what A'shai didn't know was that parks had a closing time. I looked around to see why he stopped the truck in front of one of the entrances to the park. We were supposed to be going out, so I wasn't sure why he unbuckled his seat belt.

"Ummm… you don't see that the park is closed? It's almost ten o'clock at night."

"Again, I do whatever I want." A'shai got out of the truck and pushed the swing divider out the way that was supposed to keep people like him out. He jumped back in the truck, pulled through, stopped again, jumped out, and closed it, like somebody couldn't do the same thing he did, and I was pretty sure every park had security.

"So you about to take me in the woods to kill me or something?" I started to get a little paranoid. Maybe it was the weed, I didn't know.

We parked in front of a cliff overlooking the whole town of Paterson. The park was dark; all you could see was the city lit up. A'shai turned off the truck, let down the windows, and reached for the blunt.

"I don't like being around people."

"How do you date?"

"I don't." The pulls he was taking off the blunt brought out the Mafioso in him.

"What you doing out with me then?" Inquiring minds wanted to know.

"To get some pussy." Only a real ass dude would admit that. And speaking of pussy, mine got wet after he told me what it really was.

"How you know I'm giving you some?" I tried to sound convincing. I bit my bottom lip, which probably was a dead giveaway.

"Whatever my dick wants, it gets." A'shai's eyes were tantalizingly low.

His confidence switched on a light, on a pathway to my pussy lips. I didn't know if my eyes were playing tricks on me, but it looked like his dick jumped in his pants.

"Just like a nigga. You take me on a cheap date and demanding pussy." I had to recollect myself. I didn't want him thinking I was easy. I was sexually free, but you had to work for this punani.

"Well this ain't what that is, but I'll let you make up whatever you want in your head."

"Why you always so grumpy?"

"I'm not grumpy. I speak to life differently. Not everybody been through what I been through." He passed me the blunt.

"I guessssss... Sometimes you can come off as an asshole."

"Only to the ones who don't understand my breed." The night air sat on the other side of each window. The warm breeze was our company just as much as the cicadas, crickets, grasshoppers, and katydids.

This wasn't the night I was expecting, but it was chill. Who knew all I needed was a blunt and back and forth conversation. These past few weeks had been hectic with the planning of this pre-fundraising gala. I'd been working non-stop making calls, answering emails, and getting things in order for my best friend's big day.

"I thought you would be mad about me having to cancel last week."

"I don't get mad, I get even," A'shai reassured me. I rolled my eyes.

"Anyway, the next few weeks are about to be bananas."

"You said you were planning for a big event. How's that going?"

Let me find out he was interested in my day to day. That's cute.

"It's been coming together. The Metropolitan Museum is putting a lot of money into this event. They even hired a security firm to protect and secure the paintings they're importing."

"Oh shit."

"I know, right. It's going to be locked down like a fortress." The team of four guards cost the museum close to $50,000.

"I did some security work back in the day, so let me know if you need me to look at the blueprint on the whole setup." A'shai offered his assistance.

"I'll let you know." I might just take him up on his offer, to take some things off my plate.

"Let me ask you something. Do you get that pussy waxed?" I was completely caught off guard by A'shai's questioning.

"Huh?" I had to make sure I was hearing him right.

"Take off your pants and let me handle the wetness between your legs. You can keep your heels on, just don't scratch the roof of my truck." A'shai's large hands met the bottom of his shirt, and he pulled it over his head. His muscles hugged his wife beater, and I could only imagine how it looked under it.

A'shai waited, giving me the opportunity to consent, which I respected. I guided my hands down his chest until I got to his belt, praying the player's prayer that his dick size matched his energy. Before I had a chance to find out, A'shai sat up and grabbed me around my neck. His lip and hand coordination were in sync. His lips roughly met mine, putting my body on high alert. He unbuttoned my pants, zipped down my zipper, and had them at my ankles, along with my panties. I kept my heels on as instructed.

"Open up for me."

I spread my legs wider as he rubbed up and down the opening of my lower lips. A'shai reached for my shirt and pulled down my strapless bra with ease. The warmth of his mouth met my nipple as his finger met my wetness. I gasped, having to get used to his big finger as he rotated it to the motion of my ocean. I grabbed his head, encouraging him to show the other nipple some love. That only lasted for a few seconds.

"Get out the truck." I was too far gone to contest. He pulled my door handle and was able to push the door open for me. He then leaned back over to get out on his side. I pulled my bra and shirt over my head, and I got out to see what A'shai wanted.

I strutted to the front of the truck in my red bottoms and my birthday suit. My knees buckled at A'shai stroking his abnormally large and long black anaconda. His red and black Jordan 1's was the only thing he was wearing. He was too gangsta to have a pretty dick, but I was sure he knew how to use it. I wasn't going to underestimate him this time; I was going with my gut. I wanted to touch it and stroke it for myself.

It couldn't even fit in my hands, but I did my best trying to stroke it.

It got a soft moan out of A'shai.

Here we were in the middle of the park, in front of his jeep, about to break all types of laws. A'shai picked me up and put me on the hood. He opened my legs, and his tongue added to the wetness from what his fingers did earlier. Both of my hands met the side of his head as he used verbal expression to talk to my sensitive area. He had my head spinning. I was trying to catch my breath. His tongue was lethal. With the addition of his two fingers, my body convulsed, with another nut building up right after.

"Talk… talk that… talk that shit now," A'shai said through the sucking and circular motions he was doing around my clit.

I was at the brink of an orgasm. This one felt different than the last one.

"I want this… pussy… I want it to cum… right now." I bucked against his face so he couldn't say anymore. Knots built up in my stomach, and it flooded like it was hurricane season.

I couldn't even catch my breath before A'shai grabbed me off the hood, turned me around on my heels, and drilled his massive dick in this good good. He got lost in it. My hands gripped the hood for support when A'shai grabbed my waist, sexing me at a steady pace. The pain from his rough entrance and the pounding he was now putting down turned into pleasure.

I was pretty sure I was about to pass out.

"Didn't I tell you we was going to show you?" A'shai was deep in it.

He then slowed it down. His pumps were deliberate with force, almost hitting my head with every thrust he was giving to my guts. My cries and moans echoed throughout the park. I was coming up on my second orgasm of the night, and from the sounds of it, A'shai wasn't too far behind. He wrapped his arm around my neck, pulling my back to his chest. I was now throwing it back to the rhythm of his cadence.

"I'm cum… I'm cumminggggg!" This one topped that last one.

"I am, too!" A'shai busted and collapsed on top of me on his hood.

"Excuse me, you guys have to leave." A voice snapped us out of our own reality.

A'shai's gun was pointed at the person before he had a chance to say another word. I didn't even see or knew he had a gun until the light shined in our direction.

Damn! We got caught by the park security.

MONA LISA SUTTON

MEGA WASN'T the only one who knew how to show a person a good time. I had something up my sleeve for him on his lunch. He was always busy at the shop, but he made sure to block out time to catch a breather. Today, we were going on an adventure, and I was sure he would love it. Honestly, I was a little nervous because what if he didn't like it? I was starting to learn more about Mr. Mega Dakar, but I had a long way to go. Half of our time was spent rocking each other's world. I could pick his body out of a line up, from the neck down at this point. I was becoming more and more familiar with his breathing patterns, while he was deep in it. I even knew what made him moan.

"I'm on my way out. Do you need anything?"

Gina sat at the front desk looking like a truck ran over her.

"I need a bed so I can dream about last night all over again." Gina laid her head back on her desk chair reminiscing, adding her own experience to the Mary J. Blige song. Last night, she took a ride on that pony and jumped on it like Ginuwine described.

"You shouldn't have been up doing the nasty, with your gross self. You better be glad I didn't have to bail you out of jail." Gina told me what her night entailed. I wasn't mad at her. A'shai was a fine specimen, but he looked very mean. He was always serious. The way she described her night, it was both cringe worthy and intriguing. It was like watching hardcore porn play out on the TV of my brain.

"I know you ain't talking. At this point, you are the leader of the Nasty Bitches Club. Need I remind you about your back blowing sessions you probably had right in this very space." Gina looked around the art gallery. "Please tell me you cleaned up your booty juice off my desk. Wait, did you let Mega dick bend you over up here?" She held up her hands, looking around her desk for any residue.

Flashbacks of Mega holding me above his head, giving me head, was still sketched in my brain.

"How your blog tag says, 'girl, don't trip', but you still trippin'?" We laughed at that.

"That's meant for bitches like you who get all worked up over nothing. You're the one sitting here stalling like you don't have a dick appointment right now. Forget about me. I'll be good. Go get you some dick NyQuil, and maybe it will put you to sleep so you can enjoy some good night's sleep."

"For your information, dick is not on the menu this afternoon."

"It sucks to be you."

"Girl, bye! I'll keep you posted on my ETA." I grabbed up my brown MCM monogram print shopper bag.

"I'm sure you'll tell me all the other details as well." Gina winked and got back to work.

I made my way out of the art gallery. I traded in my heels for a cute pair of vintage Burberry checked sneakers. My hair was even pulled up in a ponytail. I was relaxed today since we'd been ripping and running around. We still had a laundry list of things to do, but I was confident that it would get done. Aside from the late hours both Gina and I put into being catered to, we put just as many hours into making my first major event a success. That girl had my back.

All of the barbers' chairs in Major Cutz were filled except for the VIP chair off to the back. Instead of asking the other barbers where their boss was, I made my way to the back. The butterflies that came along with whatever connection Mega and I had was annoying. It was so childish, and it had to stop. I walked down the long hallway, passing the bathroom in search of the muffled voices I heard, which got a little clearer as I got closer.

"She's my responsibility. You don't have to worry about her." I knew Mega's voice anywhere.

"My worry is you, not her." That had to be A'shai.

"I know how to separate the two." I made out Mega's voice; he was reassuring A'shai.

They were both speaking in hushed tones. I had to take

a closer look to make sure there wasn't a *her* in the office with them. As luck would have it, when I tried to look through the small opening in the door, my head pushed the door open a little, getting the attention of both Mega and A'shai's gun. I jumped back, scared as hell that my life was over. All they had to do was pull the trigger.

"Mo Love, what are you doing here?" Mega quickly put away his gun.

I never saw a real gun before, and I never had one staring back at me. "I came to take you out for lunch." I stuttered, trying to get the words to flow right. Mega forced a smile.

"A'shai was just leaving." Mega dapped A'shai up. "I'll catch you later, A." A'shai couldn't even look my way as he passed by. I didn't know what his problem was, but he was rude.

"Did I interrupt something?" I stood, looking confused after feeling the energy in the room.

"Nope. I was helping A'shai understand some things, that's all." Mega grabbed me up in his arms and put a kiss on my forehead.

A part of me didn't know what to believe. I was split between feeling like something wasn't right, and I was also talking myself off the ledge of self-sabotage. Mega hadn't given me any reason to not trust him, so I'd give him the benefit of doubt. My eyes and ears were going to stay open, but if I could be honest, a wall went up to protect myself, just in case shit didn't pan out the way I hoped and prayed it would. At this point, I was deep in it with Mega. I gave him my body, and it would be hard to shake him.

"I hope you're not scared of heights." My intention was to change the mood.

"Scared or scary is not in my vocabulary." I could tell his curiosity was aroused.

"I'm calling your bluff. Let's go." I grabbed his hands as he grabbed his keys, and we made our way to the exit of the barbershop.

"Matt, I'll be back. If I'm not back by the time my next client is here, have Char wash the client's hair and have him ready when I get back." Mega barked his orders and with that, we were on our way.

"I don't know if your big ass can even fit in my Kia." I laughed, taking in his big frame, measuring him with my eyes. When he saw my candy apple red Kia Stinger Coupe, he quickly turned around, walking in the opposite direction.

"Whatttt?" I cracked up laughing, chasing after him.

"I'm not getting in that little ass car, yo." He chuckled.

"At least let me drive so I can keep the surprise a surprise until we get there." We made it to his Range Rover. He stopped and stared at me.

"You better be glad I like you." He passed me the smart key.

"Ayeeeeeee! I always wanted to drive a Range Rover." I hurried before he changed his mind and jumped in the driver seat. I pushed to start the truck, and it roared with power.

"I never been in the passenger seat of my own whip." He looked misplaced.

"Not even with your fiancée?" I watched as the blood drained from his face and probably his body.

Silence.

"I'm sorry. I didn't mean to get too personal." Everybody grieved differently, so I wasn't sure what part of the spectrum Mega was on.

"Outside of A'shai, I haven't talked about Mya with anyone." Mega was focused on the highway before us. "To answer your question though, nah. I was the chauffeur. She had a license but barely used it." Mega's smile turned into a chuckle and a shake of his head.

"I know that's right. That's how a queen should be treated. Look at me, now I'm your chauffeur. And we have just arrived at our destination."

"Okay, I see you." The iFLY Indoor Skydiving came into view. Mega was rubbing his hands together.

"Let's hope this vertical wind tunnel could hold such a strong man like yourself." I put the car in park and rubbed all over his body. Mega started loosening his belt.

"We won't make it in there if you don't stop rubbing up on me." I couldn't help it, so I kissed him. My whole body vibrated from the shock of our mouths connecting. I quickly pulled away, remembering the assignment.

"Let's go, boy. We have reservations, and you gotta get back to the shop." I turned off the truck, jumped out, and got ready for this rush. As soon as Mega made his way over to me, he grabbed me up.

"I'm a grown ass man. Don't ever refer to me as a boy."

"Ummm… okay."

He started tickling me like we were two high school kids. I was laughing so hard Mega couldn't help but laugh himself. We made our way inside, checked-in, and we waited to be called. Mega held me at his side as we looked on at others as they attempted to soar in the air. I was trying to understand these feelings that took over me. This felt right, but how could it be? I didn't know this man. All I knew was the bits and pieces he told me. He talked more to my inner workings than he actually talked about himself.

The wait wasn't long. Of course I had to go first. The gentleman in Mega wouldn't have it any other way. My first attempt at hitting the pocket of air was an epic fail. On the second try, I flowed for a minute or so. The third time was a charm. Oh my God! I was really up in the air. This was super dope. I kept trying until my time was up. Mega was up next, and he had to show me up. As soon as he started on the first try, he got it. With all the solid muscle weight he had, he still was able to balance himself. This was different and out of the norm, and it worked.

"Yo, you got that off. We going real skydiving next?" The look of fun Mega had in his eyes made me smile, knowing I had a part to play in it.

"You done lost your mind. Now you pushing it," I had to let Mega know. He thought it was so funny.

"We got about ten more minutes. Come with me." Mega grabbed my hand and led me toward the restroom area. We walked through the doors of the men's bathroom. My mouth was wide open. Mega did not care. Thankfully, the bathroom was empty. We went into the last stall. As soon as the stall door closed and locked, Mega began kissing me like this was the last kiss we would ever have. Only his lips could create the puddle that soaked the lining of my jeans.

Mega used his hands to unbuckle my pants. He slid them down and picked me up to slide one side of my pants leg off. I hurried to take off my panties. At the same time, Mega pulled his pants and briefs down. I just knew he was about to hit it from the back, but I was sadly mistaken. He gripped me by my waist before I had a chance to show him my backside and lifted me up. My arms locked around his head, and his dick entered my opening. His strong arms were holding me up as we found our pace.

"That's what I'm talking about. Grind on that shit." I guessed Mega didn't care that we were in a public bathroom. He wasn't loud, but if somebody walked in, they would definitely hear us. Mega wanted me to join in on the fun because the feel good sounds bounced off the stall and bathroom walls.

"Oh my God. This shit feels so good. You hitting my spot!" I let out.

"Not if you talking, I'm not. I want you speechless." His strokes got rougher.

"I see you want to take me higher than we just were. Damn, you know what you doing." I bounced up and down his shaft.

"My pussy dripping, ain't it though." After hearing Mega call it his pussy, it wasn't no need in holding my waterfall.

"Yes, your pussy dripping, Mega."

We were in the same lane, at the same speed, about to reach our destination. A detonator went off, and we both exploded. Mega still managed to hold me tight as we both caught our breath. I no longer feared that he would drop me. He had proven that he could hold a big girl like me. And he looked good doing it. We finally gathered ourselves enough to get dressed and get back to our real lives. What if this wasn't a fairytale? What if this could be real life? Good pipe would make you forget that everything was all good, until it wasn't.

MEGA DAKAR

My days were filled with clients, and my nights were filled with the unparalleled perfection of Miss Mona Lisa Sutton. She had become a part of my everyday routine, and I couldn't be more content. The more I was around Mona, the more I realized how much I missed companionship and the love I once experienced. By no means was I comparing the two; I just didn't think I would ever fall in love with another person. If Mona kept treating me like a king, I was well on my way to uncovering the true definition of a deep devotion.

Today wasn't any different. I was closing the shop and heading right over to the art gallery. Mona was super busy, and I was trying to keep her mind from going crazy. This was a big event for her, and my goal was to be her peace in any way I could, which was a little hard knowing what I knew and what I had to do. My increased feelings for her showed, but could they stand the test of time? I wasn't sure, and I would soon find out if my plan would keep everything intact. I locked up and made my way a few doors down.

We were weeks from the event, and the closer we got to the day, the more Mona and I connected. We texted, had brief phone calls, and even FaceTimed whenever we had a chance. This would technically be our last night together before I had to do the unthinkable. I wanted to leave Mona room to be the boss she was and get ready for the biggest night of her career. I also wanted to solidify the plans with A'shai and get in the right frame of mind without distraction. Tonight was crucial for so many reasons, but my main objective was to create a space of peace and tranquility for Mona.

"I feel like I haven't hugged you in forever."

Mona grabbed onto me the moment she was close enough to touch me. I was able to find her in her office, doing what she did best.

"You were just in my arms last night, Mo Love, but I miss you, too." It wasn't something I was just saying; it was straight facts.

"I wish I could have woken up in your arms."

It left Mona's lips before her brain caught up to what she said. It was her true feelings, and I knew it would resurface again.

"I'm sorry," she continued. "It's just that, I don't know if you'll ever be completely over losing your ex-fiancée. It's not like you are seeking help or talking through it with someone. How can you heal from something you don't express?"

Mona pulled back from our embrace as we both stood looking at one another.

"Talking has never been me. Who was I going to express myself to?" I paused, although we both knew it was a rhetorical question. "The world doesn't listen to men like me, who came from the gutter. I didn't have time to talk about my feelings. Not only was I in the battlefield of my mind, but I was also at war with my reality." This was the most I had expressed in a long time, and I owed a lot of that to Mona.

"Did you talk to Mya, Mega? Like, really open up about the things your thoughts whisper to you that nobody hears?"

Mona took a second before continuing.

"You are a great man... Nah, scratch that; you are a phenomenal man who has always been the fixer, while you covered up the holes in your structure to help others rebuild."

I couldn't say a word; I took it all in.

In between our mental processing of the conversation, I was able to grab her up and put her on the edge of her desk as I slid between her legs to allow her to lay her head on my chest.

She listened to my heartbeat as I caressed her uneasiness without saying a word. I was most definitely going to answer her question. I just needed some time to gather my words. I couldn't shoot my way out of this one or even buy the perfect words to say. I had to dig deep to express what made me, me.

"Things like this take time for someone like me. I done lost too much, too soon, and I've seen too much to be optimistic. I think the worst first and still look for it when it's not present. So, telling you or anybody else about those whispers will only alarm you, not protect you."

Mona met me at a different time in my life, where I was a little more tamed than I once was, so there weren't too many dark convictions at this point that I could confess.

"Do you trust me?"

Mona's words were in sync with the beat of my heart.

"I trust you; I just don't want to lose you." Those were my feelings put on display. I couldn't say it any differently.

"I can see how you grouped trust and loss together. Just hearing some of your story told me all I needed to know. I'm here to tell you that the new chronicle being written will read better than the chapters before it. Your life's biography deserves new chapters filled with love, laughter, and everything else in between."

Mona's words gave me a bitch ass fluttery sensation that hit the pit of my stomach.

Is this love?

To have someone leave their world of chaos and the things they had going on, to come see about me, was priceless. It was something money couldn't buy, and to have experienced it twice in a lifetime showed me there was hope for the lost. When two worlds collided and could coexist in the same space, it became the land of the free and the home of the brave. If I had a choice, I would live in this world we created forever, but that wasn't guaranteed, especially after the dirty deed that was standing in my way of me being totally unchained.

"This new chapter with you has brought the softer side of me out. These last three years have been a blur. It's been non-stop work and no play. That was the way I grieved—that's what kept me afloat because I was drowning." Hearing it leave my mouth made me feel weak, which caused me to pause, but I needed to continue. "From a youngin', I had to write my own story. My mother's pen wasn't consistent, and my dad lost his pen all together which left empty chapters for my character. I learned how to create my own book, whether I had a publisher or not." I was the author and finisher of my fate.

"Where can I buy a signed copy of your book, Mr. Dakar, so I could read it under the stars?" We both laughed.

"Come on. Grab your stuff, lock up, and come with me." I kissed Mona's forehead as she looked up at me from her seated position on her desk. I moved from between her legs to let her get up. "I got you. Let's go." I was now eager to show her what I had in mind for tonight.

Our destination for the night was the newest marina in Brooklyn Bridge Park, where we found a parking space and made our way to the 46' Searay Flybridge Yacht that was ready to take us to the best locations in New York. I scheduled us for a scenic skyline tour of Downtown and Midtown Manhattan. Mona's eyes lit up with a sparkle that showed her appreciation for our night cap. Frank Ocean's version of "At Your Best (You Are Love)" was playing on the loudspeakers of the yacht. Mona grabbed my hand tighter as we made our way on the boat.

"Mr. Dakar, welcome to the Searay Flybridge. I'll be your captain this evening. My name is Robert, and my job is to drive while you enjoy the nice breeze and scenery that surrounds us. Everything you have requested is on board. You won't have to worry about anything. Tonight is about the two of you, the music, and the ocean rocking back and forth."

The captain showed us to the front of the boat, where there was a laying area, and I helped Mona take off her shoes to get comfortable. We had drinks on ice and a little nice blanket and pillow setup. Once we were good, the captain sailed away on the blue waters.

"You said you wanted to read under the stars, right?" I looked on at Mona as she surveyed the sky. It was lit up with little fluorescent snowflakes that were aligned in the still of the night. This was peace; it was a reminder that even in darkness, you can see some light, some glimmer of hope somewhere in every situation. I was always fascinated with the way the sky looked at night.

"I have never experienced life to this magnitude. You've taken me on dates to places that didn't exist until I met you. You've set the bar high for what's to come. Are you sure this is what you want?"

Mona grabbed her drink and leaned back on the pillow.

"That isn't evident in my actions?" It was my turn to get relaxed for this ride.

"Words of affirmation are at the top of my love language list."

I guess that was Mona's way of answering no.

"That would be something I would have to work on. I'm a doer. Words aren't proven; it's in one's actions that yields results. Now that I know that's important to you, I'll be sure to affirm you verbally as well as take the initiative to show you." Mona was worth it, and it didn't hurt to try.

Tonight, we were going to let the waves guide our conversation to depths unknown. They said getting to know someone was the best part of a relationship, and that was exactly why we were enjoying it. If you would have told me I'd be here a few months ago, I wouldn't have believed it. It was crazy how things could change in an instant without even realizing it. That was when you knew it was organic and meant to be.

"I'm still waiting."

I guessed my answer wasn't what Mona wanted to hear.

"This is what I want. I wouldn't be here if I didn't think you were worth it. You are beautiful, you are brilliant, and I salute you for your strength and determination. You are one of a kind, and I'm thankful to have gotten to know you." I could go on and on, but that was what came from the heart.

"See, that wasn't so hard." Mona smiled, turned, and kissed me on the cheek. Alex Isley's "Under the Moon" was now playing.

"I feel like we have talked about some heavy stuff, but I still don't know what your favorite color is," Mona observed.

"I know your favorite color." This was when I showed her I was a man who paid attention.

"What is it?" I knew she would ask that next.

"It's black. You don't only like the color; you love the race and what we stand for," I said without hesitation.

"How you know that?" she questioned, shocked that I knew.

"I'm starting to learn more about you each day we spend together." I could point out a lot, but she asked the question.

"If I would have to guess, I would say your favorite color is... green!"

Mona shouted, excited that she may have it right.

"Oh my God, how did you know that!" I mocked her excitement, causing us to both burst out laughing.

"Shut up." Mona playfully hit me in my chest as I lay back and continued to laugh.

We got quiet for a minute, took in the scenery, and let the music serenade us. Different thoughts invaded our minds as we tried to piece together our feelings. That was our way of being caught up in the moment—taking in everything that came with our togetherness. I looked over at Mona as she surveyed the sky and what it had to offer. Her beauty was undeniable, and her smile was so contagious that it had me overjoyed. I felt I hit the jackpot for way more than I put in.

MONA LISA SUTTON

She's a bad mama jama.
Just as fine as she can be.

I SANG the lyrics to Mr. Carl Carton while doing a walkthrough of the minor renovations that were taking place. The museum had certain requirements that weren't at any cost to me. The music blasted through the gallery speakers, while everybody got to work. Gina was in the back receiving orders, and I was on cloud nine, loving what I was seeing. Smelling Mega's cologne on me when he hadn't even been around today, I knew I had to be buggin'. I was glad I had something to distract me, although I did find myself lost in a moment of him, of us in the short time we had together.

Dreams did come true, and life could take a turn at any

moment. Who would've thought I would be here two years ago? I looked at the exhibit area that my and Mega's paintings would be, the night of the pre-fundraising gala. I was nervous but excited to share the moment with another introverted artist. I never wanted to be mainstream. All I wanted to do was what I loved.

"When this is all said and done, I'm going to need a vacation," Gina made known once we met back up in front of the gallery.

"You and me both." I high fived her, letting her know she wasn't the only one.

"You missing Mega?" That was mad random. With Gina, it was a reason she was asking.

"I've been so busy these last three weeks that we barely had a chance to kick it. The last time we really went out or had any alone time was when we went to the marina."

"What I'm hearing is you dick deprived. Shit, girl, I am, too."

"Oh, so you telling me A'shai hasn't been over putting marks on your body from the rough sexy y'all be having?"

"How, bitch? I've been here with your ass." Gina rolled her eyes.

"I'm sorry. I know we've put in a lot of hours." I was thankful for everything that Gina was doing.

"There's no need to apologize. I love what I do, and the money is not too shabby, either." We both laughed.

The front door to the gallery swung open. Both men walked in, and it seemed like everything stopped around me. The theme music that happened to be playing on the speakers was perfect. The Game's "This is How we Do" was the background music as Gina and I almost drooled at how fine they both were. They were basically the same height. You could tell they were brothers, even if they weren't blood. That was how strong their connection was.

"This corny ass dude made me do it," A'shai spoke first.

"Do what?" Gina and I spoke in unison.

"We catered lunch for you and your team. The food truck is parked outside."

"I told him you must have some good pussy." I covered my mouth, embarrassed by A'shai's comment. A laugh followed not too far after.

"You ain't know? We the pussy fairies. We got you sprung off in the springtime."

"You better tell them, best friend." Our hands cosigned our agreement.

Mega and A'shai both looked at each other, with a brotherly smirk and a confident head shake. They weren't convinced, I was guessing. Yeah, we were giving up the drawers, but they kept coming back for more, so it had to be some truth to that. I was sure they could get it from anywhere, but they chose to take a dip in our oceans. We weren't exclusive, so I didn't know who they were giving their pipe to. I'd save the "what are we doing" conversation for after this event. My feelings couldn't take it anymore. Things like this kept me believing that there were some good men left in the world.

"Your staff can go outside, and Chef Travis will take their orders." Mega gave instructions on how this was going to work. "We already put y'all orders in."

"You don't know what I like. What kind of food is it anyway?" Gina was a picky eater.

"It's soul food, and you're gonna taste whatever I give you." A'shai stared at Gina and challenged her.

"Man, we ordered everything he had on the menu, so you have choices," Mega corrected A'shai.

"Thank you, Mega. Your brother is about to get these hands, he keeps playing with me." Gina got into a boxing stance and was fighting the air. "I'm tired of him talking to me like he owns me." Gina playfully hit A'shai in his chest.

"Ouch," A'shai said dryly without flinching.

We all enjoyed a laugh together.

I made my rounds, telling the staff that they could go outside for lunch to eat at Betty Jean's Soul Truck. They were excited for free food and probably more excited about getting a break. We'd been going hard since seven a.m. this morning. I was thankful for my team, and this was a great way to thank them. It had been on my heart to treat them to something, and Mega beat me to it. Why was this man so good to me? That was a question I couldn't seem to get out of my brain. It was stuck on the closing credits of each one of our encounters.

While the staff was outside, the four of us went into the breakroom, and we were brought our food. We sat around chatting it up and laughing, mostly at Gina and A'shai going back and forth. It was like they were in competition with their mouths. The food was good, but I broke my diet. I had to get in this dress for the gala. I didn't want to seem ungrateful, so I went against my better judgment and dug in.

"You like it?" Mega whispered to me while Gina and A'shai were debating something.

"Yes. This is not my cheat day, though."

"It's only one meal. You'll bounce back, Mo Love. Your body is the business, anyway." Mega moisturized his lips, feeling on my body like Gina and A'shai weren't sitting across from us. Physical touch had become my love language ever since I felt Mega's big hands roam my body. The more we were together, the more he continued to bring things out of me. He was the inspiration for the painting I'd be sharing with the world.

"Why, thank you. Your body is not too bad, either, if I must say so myself." I laid my hand on his most prized possession. Mega made it jump, and when he did, my clit responded.

"Damn, let me find out Mega done pulled out his dick over there." Gina eyed us suspiciously.

"Why you worried about his nut? You should be worried about yours." A'shai fondled Gina's titty, and she gasped and threw her head back. She gathered herself quickly though.

"Are y'all coming to the gala next week?" Gina tried her hardest to move on from A'shai's foreplay, but you could tell it was hard.

"I'm going to be here as the owner's plus one," Mega answered Gina's question. She already knew that because I told her. I guessed that was her way of seeing if A'shai would be tagging along.

"A'shai, what about you?" My guess was right.

"I don't attend corny shit with corny people. A crowded place is not my thing. So it's a no for me, dawg."

"Wait, so you calling us corny?" Gina wouldn't let up with the questions.

"If you corny, say it without saying it." A'shai put in a counteroffer.

"This is too much." I laughed out loud.

"How's the planning been going?" Mega followed suit with changing the topic.

"It's going well, actually. We have a few more days of getting stuff in order. Before you know it, the day will be here." I was excited to share this part of me with someone outside of Gina.

"A'shai, I was telling Mona that you did some security work before," Gina let be known.

Mega almost choked on his water. It seemed to have gone down the wrong pipe.

"My bad. I was drinking that water too fast." Mega gathered himself.

"Yeah, mostly at the strip clubs. I had to make sure nobody stole fake booty cheeks and silicone." A'shai was too funny.

"If you were coming, I would have had you as extra eyes. It's always good to work with people you trust." There weren't too many that wore that trust title.

"Unfortunately, I have other plans. If something changes between now and then, I'll tell Gina while I'm stroking and poking." Gina playfully smacked A'shai across his chest.

"Speaking of stroking something, we'll be back." Mega's hand met mine, and he pulled me up and out the breakroom doors.

"I'm locking this door. Bend that ass over," I overheard A'shai tell Gina before I was out of hearing range.

We continued down the hall to my office. As soon as the door closed and locked, I jumped on Mega. I didn't have to wait for him; I wanted it just as bad as he did. He knocked everything off my desk and laid me flat on my back. Without breaking the kiss, our lips didn't want to depart from the pleasure they were getting. Once we came up for air, I pushed Mega off me. He had a confused look on his face. He was rock hard; his jeans had no more room to hold it. I made my way over to him, undid his belt, and dropped his drawers. He was heavy to move, but he worked with me. Mega was now on the desk.

My body fit so perfectly between his legs. I leaned forward to say hello to Mega's standing soldier. My grip was gentle but firm. My hands started doing an up and down motion. If it wasn't rock hard before, it was brick from my touch. I leaned over with an urgency to lick the tip in a circular motion. Without warning, I put my wet mouth around it, not being able to go all the way down. I added just enough spit, getting the hang of it. I looked up as I was going to town on Mega's magical tool.

"That's what I'm talking about. I see you trying to make me cum." He was enjoying the action I was giving him, and I was, too.

I spoke with my mouth all the things I couldn't say, for

all the times he had me crawling the walls. Mega's tongue was satan himself. It was time for me to show him he deserved to be treated like a king. I hoped he felt it, from his head to his toes and then back up to the animal I held in my hands. I was singing with it like we were on the stage at the Grammys. I was giving the performance of a lifetime, and the best part was about to happen.

"Yo, I'm about to cum." Mega's hands met the top of my head. "Oh shit, Mo Love. Damn." His hips started to meet the rotation of my mouth and hands. I didn't know where more spit came from, but it shined all around.

"Here it is… Oh shit." I jerked until the pipe burst all on my hands and mouth.

I hurried and got something to wipe my mouth and hands. Mega didn't care. He got up to put his semi-erect penis back in its resting place.

"I ain't know you had that in you." Mega was drained, trying to get his strength back.

"You don't know a lot of things." We were still getting to know each other.

"I like what I've learned so far, no bullshit." I would say that was game, but we were way past that.

"You're an interesting character yourself." I got myself together in the office mirror. I did have to go back to work.

"I'm the best character you'll meet." Mega came and stood behind me in the mirror. He was a giant compared to me. We looked good though. "Let's go."

Mega unlocked the door, and we walked out in the hallway. A'shai was coming out of the breakroom at the same time. We made it to the breakroom, Mega gave me a kiss, then kept walking. A'shai followed behind him. Gina and I stood in the doorway watching them walk out. They pounded fists, making their way out the door. Did we just get played?

Metropolitan Museum of Art
Pre-fundraising Gala

WHEN I SAID I did this thing, I did it. We pulled up to the red carpet that was in front of the art gallery in a Rolls-Royce Wraith. I was pulling up with the owner of The Picturesque Art Gallery, and the way we looked together, we had to step out in nothing but the best. My royal printed, champagne and black tuxedo went well with Mona's black sheer gown with lace decals.

The walkway was decorated with a backdrop, and there were lights, cameras, and people to match. My stomach started doing flips. I didn't know how this would play out. I thought we had a solid plan in play. I looked over at Mona, who was looking amazingly beautiful. Her hair was up, so you could really see all the flawless features of her face. Her makeup was perfect, although I lived for her natural look. No makeup and her curls showed that skin deep beauty that you couldn't buy. Tonight, the inner fight to not break Mona's heart grew stronger.

It was all or nothing.

The valet attendant opened the door to the Wraith. I stepped out, and all the cameras were on me, flashing like I was a celebrity. Usually, I would lay low, but there was a method to my madness. If I wanted to keep kicking it with Mona and see where things went, I had to stick to the plan. I made my way to the driver's side to open the door for the baddest female out here tonight. As we made our way to the red carpet, Mona stopped and posed for pictures, so I had no choice.

"Hey, girl!" Gina rushed toward us. She wasn't looking too bad herself.

"You did it. You really did this shit, sis'. I'm so proud of you." Gina hugged Mona. They started jumping up and down, still embracing with love. The camera caught every moment.

"Don't make me cry. You know I've been holding in these tears all day."

"Mega, I hope you brought a handkerchief. It's going to be a lot of tears." I was shook for a moment. Why did I feel like I would be the cause of those tears, and not in a good way?

There were two armed security guards in view, one on the red carpet and one at the front door that I peeped while pulling up.

"Mega! Did you hear me?" Gina's loud mouth brought me back from my observation.

"You already know I got her." I was sure of that, but after tonight, I wasn't sure if she'd feel the same way.

Man, I didn't know. I never felt this way about a job before. I didn't know if it was because I was falling in love with Mona, or if it was something else. Ruby had been radio silent, and so had the black Impala. Only time would tell what we were up against. At this point, we were playing the waiting game. Either way, we were going to get this painting to Gavino tonight at Teterboro airport. We didn't want war with the Italians. They were deep in numbers, so I had to keep our binding agreement.

"You better walk this red carpet, bitch, and let them see you work." Gina snapped three times going up and down, whatever that meant. They parted ways by kissing each cheek, and Gina went back to her duties. We began to walk the rest of the red carpet toward the entrance.

"What brings you here tonight, and you are wearing that dress?" The interviewer held the mic up, and the camera was on Mona.

"I am here to celebrate black art, by showcasing some talented African American artists that you will never forget after tonight."

"For the first time in decades, they are showing the Maurizio Contini painting. How exciting is that?"

Contini?

"I'm super excited that they chose to bring such a groundbreaking piece of art back to life through the space I created. I haven't gotten a chance to see it myself. They had it under lock and key, so I'll be seeing it up close and personal with everyone in attendance."

If my memory served me right, Gavino's last name was Contini. I didn't even think to ask the name of the painting. I just needed pictures. It wasn't what they hyped it up to be. Gavino did say it was a family heirloom, but I didn't think it had his last name attached to it. There had to be a reason it was no longer in the possession of the Contini family. Shit wasn't adding up.

"What's your name, beautiful soul?" the reporter asked.

"My name is Mona Lisa Sutton, and I'm the owner of The Picturesque. I want to thank each and every one who donated to make this night a success. We still have more money to raise." Mona held on to me the whole interview.

"And who is this handsome man with you tonight?" Mona looked at me with a wide smile that showed great happiness.

"I'm her boyfriend. I'm here to celebrate her for all her accomplishments. She's out here doing it, and I am so proud of her." I kissed Mona as a seal to the deal.

"Ms. Mona Lisa, what was your prayer? I needs me one of him." We all laughed, even the cameraman.

The interview ended, and we made our way past the second security guard. I looked around. Not a lot was rearranged and changed from when we stopped by with the food truck. The layout of how every painting flowed together was brilliant. Each room had about six paintings on the wall with two art sculptures in the middle. One of the six areas was blocked off with a large curtain, sealing the reveal. It was packed. The elevator music was low, but that was so everyone could network and mingle. Get that liquor up in them to spend their money. Mona and I worked the room of guests. After all, she was the hostess.

"I'll be right back," Mona said to me after introducing me to so many people.

I people watched for a few until someone came into my field of vision. Ruby always stood out in a crowd. I spoke her up, and I wished I would have never put it out there. She took her time after spotting me looking at her. Her sly smile remained until we were face to face.

"You lost your fucking mind?" I said through clenched teeth, trying my hardest to not raise my voice.

"Is that the way to talk to your mother?"

"You really been smoking drugs. I will choke your ass out, right here."

"Oh, so you're no longer holding in your hate for me?" I hated when people didn't take accountability for the part they played in the hate.

"Listen, I don't know what you think this is, but you have five minutes to make your way back out that door. If you don't, I'm going to call off the job and then feed you to the wolves that are the Italians. You're messing up money." I was seething as I shot daggers through her.

"I would love to meet Ms. Mona Lisa. You guys look good together. Where is she?"

"I see what you doing, but you don't want to go there with me. I promise you." Ruby already knew what I was capable of. She wasn't new to this.

"Get the job done." Ruby grabbed wine off the server's tray.

She lifted it in the air and walked off. I watched her like a hawk as she made her way out the front entrance.

Ruby put no fear in my heart. I knew this wasn't going to be easy. I'd rather her show her face than lurk in the shadows. She didn't do things just to do them, either. There had to be more to her showing up here. She never showed up while we were on a job. Ever. It could be a tactic to throw me off my game. I was a little shook at first, seeing her, but she would never know that. I looked around, reached in my inside suit jacket pocket, and grabbed the burner phone.

She showed.

I quickly put the phone away.

I looked around for Mona to see who stole her away. There was one security guard walking around. Most people wouldn't know that he was one, but I peeped it the moment he spoke to his hand. Fake ass secret service imposter. I spotted Mona talking with Gina and some corny, lame ass dude. He was being too touchy feely, and I wasn't having it.

I was quick on my feet, making my way over to them. Mona must have sensed me coming. She turned around, smiling brightly. Her smile caused the dude to look up as I walked between them.

"Mega, this is world famous artist, extraordinaire, Artorius Collins." I didn't even look dude's way.

"Is the DJ going to change this music?" I said to both Mona and Gina. Gina burst out laughing, an arrogant laugh that got ole boy a little bothered. You could tell it in his posture. If he felt a way about it, I dared him to say it.

"Mona, congrats again on all your success. I can't wait to work with you in the future. Maybe we can create something together." He tried to lean in for a hug.

"You reached your limit for tonight. You touch her again, I'll break your fucking arm." I moved in closer so he could look up at me. Mona quickly got between us.

"Thanks, Artorius, and thank you for donating money." Mona grabbed my hand, struggling to drag me away.

"What are you doing?" Mona probed. We stopped in a not so crowded area.

"He needs to keep his hands to himself." Point Blank.

"Mega, I can handle myself."

I just stared at her.

"And just because you said you were my boyfriend doesn't mean you are. Was that your way of asking me to be your girl, or were you acting?" I couldn't believe she was doing this here.

"I'm not about to do this with you. I want you to enjoy your night." This wasn't part of the plan. I didn't need this shit right now.

"I'm just as nervous as you." I looked at her with a confused look.

"What you mean?" I doubted if my posture showed that I was nervous. I had years of experience. There was more on the line this time around.

"For everybody to see your painting." Mona looked at me like she knew something.

"There's only one person's opinion that I care about." I pulled her close. It was the truth. I was only doing it because she asked.

"Something just vibrated." I pulled away from her, realizing it was the phone in my pocket.

"Mona, come with me. They're some people I want you to meet," Gina interrupted our conversation.

"I'm going to the bathroom." I stole a kiss before Gina pulled Mona away.

I quickly made my way toward the back. I pulled out my phone and read the text message.

Money, Power, Respect.

Is the Key To Life

WHEN THE TEXT came through almost thirty minutes later, I knew what time it was. I was in Target's parking lot, five minutes away from the action. I was dressed for the occasion. The black classic tuxedo fit me to perfection. I never did a job dressed up, with shoes and a bowtie. I needed a nice and reliable car that would get me from zero to one hundred real quick. My Lamborghini Urus SUV afforded me just that, with just enough space to secure the bag. This feeling never got old. It was now or nothing.

I checked the back before pulling off, making sure I had everything I needed.

It took a little longer than I projected, but it didn't put me behind schedule. We had a meeting time at Teterboro with Gavino for that exchange. It was going to be hard for

Mega to get away from Mona. A lot of people were expecting to see the painting that cost so much. How Mona would explain that—I didn't know. All I cared about was this money so I could start this real estate shit. If that didn't work, the streets wouldn't mind taking me back. It was a beast's nature to want to stay in the wild.

"Sir, this part of the area is closed. There is no parking back here." A security guard stopped me before pulling through the back of the shops.

"I'm working the event tonight. I have the Mega Dakar painting in the back." I pointed to the painting that Mega was debuting tonight along with Mona. I made sure not to cover it up to show proof of the amazing work of my brother's hands. There was no denying that it belonged at an event like this.

"Setup was this morning, but I'll let you and your boss deal with that." The security guard moved to the side and let me drive down the path to the gallery's back entrance. He couldn't see what was taking place from the yardage between him and The Shops at Riverside.

I pulled up and parked not too far from the door. There was another security guard with a clipboard. He was brolic as hell, standing by the closed back door. Hopefully, he wouldn't take his job too seriously tonight. I popped the trunk, getting ready to take the painting out.

"Sir, this is a restricted area. All deliveries have been received." I turned around to face him, giving him my best professional smile.

"I have the Mega Dakar painting that was just picked

up from the airport. It was delayed due to people being out with COVID." I slid on my gloves.

"I'm sorry, I can't let you in. I was told nothing goes in and out of here while the event is going on."

I pulled out my gun, silencer attached. I didn't have time for this. It was sitting right under the painting. I was hoping I didn't have to use it. It was soft ass, big niggas like this one that wanted to flex their authority. He held his hands up. I was pretty sure he was strapped, so I patted him down, looking at him the whole time. If he moved, I was going to end his life.

I felt the gun he had tucked inside his pants. As I was pulling it out, dude elbowed me in my face, making me stumble. His gun dropped to the ground, but I was able to connect with a right hook across his jaw. He was seeing stars for a few seconds, which gave me leverage. My gun was the boxing glove to my punch.

His hand met his face from the blow of the gun. He pulled a razor from his mouth, which left blood leaking from my forearm. It cut right through my suit jacket, right to my flesh. I didn't even have to react. I kicked this nigga in his nuts with my Christian Louboutin Greggo Oxfords. I took the breath right out of him, and I wasn't stopping there. I kneed him in his face as he was bent over, sending him backwards, hitting the ground. I broke his ribs with the stomping of my patent leathers. The time was ticking, but this ass whupping was warranted. He had to go.

Pop. Pop. Pop.

The gunshot was muffled by the silencer, but it did the

same damage, leaving the security guard lifeless. Fuck. Without having to think much, I quickly grabbed the guard up, dragging him closer to the truck. I pulled the painting out the trunk, ready to replace it with the body of the guard. The tarp I had for the painting that Gavino paid for would have to be the covering for top-flight security. He was heavy, but I lifted more in the gym. Once I was able to get him in and cover him up, I found something that would cover up the evident incision. I let myself in the back entrance with Mega's painting in hand. The frame it was in made it heavier than it would be hanging solo.

Boxes were everywhere in the back area of the gallery. They used it more as a supply closet. I had to get to the next room off the hallway to get to the painting. This part of the gallery should be closed off, so I was hoping that once I opened the door, it would be all clear for me to get in and out. I put my ear up to the door to see if I heard anybody, but the music and chatter sounded far away. I slowly opened the door to peek my head out, and the coast was clear.

I grabbed up the painting, closed the door behind me and made my way behind the large curtains that closed off this exhibit area. It was easy to spot the painting we had to get for Garvino; it hung on a wall, all by itself, covered by a white sheet. The painting that they had for Mega was an old painting that he used as a decoy. I laid Mega's other painting down and did some rearranging. After I was finished, Mona's painting was put under the white sheet. I replaced her slot with Mega's painting, and I grabbed up the money maker.

Every step I took, I made sure to check my

surroundings. As I got closer to the door, my heart was beating based on the fact that there was cash waiting for me. I was able to make it from the exhibit area to the hallway, and now I was pulling the tarp over the painting and the body I collected on the way. A smile crept across my face as I started the Lamborghini and pulled off.

GINA THOMPSON

IT WAS the time everyone had been waiting for, and I was super excited to finally get to this part. Mona was the one who would be introducing what was behind the black curtains. She had been practicing her speech all week. I damn near knew it by heart. Forget that Maurizio Contini painting. It was Mona's and Mega's paintings that were going to wow the audience. They showed their love through their paintings. They may have not said it to each other, but they spoke it with their paint brushes. It was so beautiful to witness, knowing where my girl came from and the things she had to do to stand on her own two feet.

"I'm going to pee on myself, Gina," Mona said, walking up to me. She looked for Mega, who was standing by her side. Something was off about him, but it didn't matter at that moment. This was Mona's moment. He was still probably in his feelings from the words he had with

Artious Collins. Mega straight punked ole boy, so I wasn't sure what the beef was.

"Girl, you got this. We done went over it a million times. You better work that spotlight and don't let it work you." Mona always needed that pep talk. Sometimes I had to talk the bad bitch out of her.

"Mo Love, you will be fine." Mega tried his best to calm Mona's shivers from her nervousness.

"What if I trip walking up to the mic?" No matter what we said, Mona was going to think of every possible bad thing that could happen. She'd always been an overthinker since we were kids.

"I'll catch you, don't worry." Mega grabbed her up in his arms.

"Give her some dick real quick to take the edge off." I looked on at the two of them. That got both of them to smile. It probably got Mona's mind off her speech. Knowing her, she was probably seeing his dick in the light.

"Why are you like this?" Mona's laugh calmed her down a little.

"This is what I'm here for." Our childhood traumas brought us together, and we'd been inseparable ever since.

When my father beat on my mother, it was Mona's house that was my safe place. When my dad was away, working his three jobs, it was my house that gave birth to the artist inside Mona. I would watch her paint for hours in my basement, thankful for the distraction. Back then, we always asked the question, why couldn't it be different? We envisioned different lives while expressing our trauma responses. Today was proof that anything could happen that you put your mind to.

"Please welcome the owner of The Picturesque Art Gallery, Ms. Mona Lisa Sutton," the announcer stated. A loud round of applause echoed through the place. Mega let Mona go into the wild with a kiss and a reassuring smile.

Mona didn't trip or pee herself. She gracefully made her way to the podium. This had been one of the greatest nights of my life, to finally see my friend in the spotlight that she deserved. Her talent wasn't based on her personality, and she wasn't born into it like Artious. Mona had skills. It had to be in her genes; she was born with it. Tonight, everyone was about to witness what I did so many times in my basement.

"Good evening, everyone, and thank you for coming out tonight. Tonight has been a dream come true, and without each and every one of you, this wouldn't be possible." Mona looked at everyone in attendance. I could hear the shake in her voice, but that was only because I knew her. She continued.

"The Picturesque Art Gallery represents the artist with no voice, the ones who are overlooked not only because of the color of their skin but where they are from. I once was imprisoned for my love of art. That's why when you first walk in, you see the young black girl on her knees praying. It was those same prayers that got me here, along with the push of my best friend and sister, Gina Thompson." The spotlight was now on me. I started hitting the Kim Parker dance from The Parkers Show. The crowd laughed.

"See y'all, she keeps me laughing, and this next person

keeps me sane." Mona took a pause. She battled in her mind if she should add Mega to her list of thank yous, but I knew she would. "This man came right on time; he pushed me to live again and celebrate my accomplishments. Tonight, he will be debuting a painting alongside myself. Can we get a round of applause for Mega Dakar, owner of Major Cutz, one of our biggest donors of the night." They gave him a round of applause.

"Many of you are here to see the Maurizio Contini painting that has not been showcased since debuting thirty years ago. To this day, no one has seen the artist that created this masterpiece. The Contini painting will live on forever with the debut of my painting and the painting of Mr. Mega Dakar. Without further ado, make some noise and put your hands together for the exhibits of the night."

What the fuck? Mona looked my way for answers.

MONA LISA SUTTON

THIS HAD to be a game that I never signed up to play. The Maurizio Contini painting was gone. It was missing, replaced with my painting. I guessed the other one was Mega's painting. I wasn't even sure who the third painting belonged to. Tears started to stream down the setting of my makeup. I couldn't understand why or how this was happening. This wasn't in the plans, or even plan B, so I wasn't sure what this was. Clapping could still be heard, but the world stopped for me. I had to explain what was going on. And how was I going to do that?

"Gina, what happened to the Maurizio Contini painting?" I was barely able to utter.

"I promise you, it was there earlier." Gina looked as confused as I did. She was usually on her game, so I didn't doubt that.

"Mo Love, are you okay?" I heard Mega, but his words didn't stop me from running to my office. It didn't make sense. The only reason the Metropolitan Museum added another night was to show the Contini painting. It arrived that day and was checked in by Gina, who I knew for sure was on point. Why would someone want a painting that only a hundred plus people saw?

It didn't make sense. I also wondered why someone would want to sabotage my career. I worked my ass off to pull this off. Maybe my dad was right; this life wasn't for me.

I made it to my office, slamming my door behind me. You could hear the music playing, which probably didn't hide the whispers. This was a disaster. The painting that I was sure was Mega's was breathtaking if my memory served me right. It was a couple, split between two worlds, coming together to paint on a blank canvas. The colors and the highlights he used for the background made the picture come alive. It was in the details of the way he outlined the two individuals. Their backs were turned as they both added something to the canvas before them.

"Smile for me. Your smile is contagious." I didn't even realize that my office door was open. Mega stood there. His eyes didn't have the sparkle I needed. It seemed forced but sympathetic.

"Everything I built just crumbled to the ground. I don't know how I am going to explain this to Michael Weiss." I was sure there was a fine attached to the missing painting.

"Who is that?"

"The president of the Mets."

"Don't worry. I'll worry about him."

Knock, knock.

Gina walked in, hesitant at first. She came in with a face towel and a bag. She looked between me and Mega.

"Wipe your face, then let me get you right real quick. Mr. Weiss wants to talk to you." I didn't know how she didn't figure that would bring more tears.

"Oh my God. I'm going to jail."

"Listen, you have no idea what just happened out there." Gina could spare me the details. I couldn't take it anymore.

"We don't care about all that." Mega read my mind.

"Mr. Weiss wants you to come out and talk to him about featuring your painting at the Met Gala tomorrow and a possible exhibit space long term." She started pulling out her makeup supplies, knowing I couldn't resist.

"Bitch, shut up! What about the Contini painting?" I started crying again, this time tears of joy.

"He's going to get his people on it. They are the ones who hired the security firm, so that's not on us."

"I want whoever did this to pay. I hope they rot in hell." I meant every word. I looked over at Mega, who was extremely quiet. Was this too much for him? I knew he didn't ask for any of this. This was all a lot to take in.

I quickly pulled myself together. My girl wouldn't steer me wrong by allowing me to show my face after what happened. Mr. Weiss must have talked a good game, unless he was trying to set me up. Either way, I was going to find out what he wanted. To think, I went back and forth about even showing the painting. It was my way of no longer being stuck as that little girl playing hide and seek, with a passion stamped from birth.

> I used our KEY!

I FINALLY HAD time to read A'shai's message.

I didn't want to seem like I was rushing, so I had to really play it cool. It hurt to see Mona break down the way she did. It worked in my favor that she got the deal of a lifetime. They even asked about my painting. I wasn't in the right frame of mind to talk business; I was already clocked in at my other job. Mona was so exhausted, I convinced Gina to take her home at the end of the night, reassuring them I'd take care of locking up and answering any questions if they came up. It didn't take long for everybody to clear out and get on their way.

It was way past midnight, and we were set to meet Gavino at the airport in about an hour. Our meeting time was at two a.m. I had to drop the Wraith off at the house.

A'shai should be pulling up right behind me. The night skies had me looking forward to the morning. A'shai pulled up in front of my house. A'shai's attire was disheveled, and he didn't look too good.

"Bro', you good?" I quickly jumped in the car as soon as I peeped his disposition.

"I'm good, I'm good." That definitely wasn't the case by the looks of it.

"I see blood. How the fuck you good?" I saw a Walmart bag with supplies to cover up a wound. I panicked. I couldn't lose A.

"I took care of it myself. I'm good." I had no choice but to believe him. I'd play along for now, but if he gave me any indication that he wasn't capable of finishing the job, I was pulling back.

"You got everything?" I already knew the answer to that. I peeped it in the back.

"Really?" A'shai's face said it all.

"What happened?" I couldn't let it go. I had to see what caused the damage.

"They had security in the back. Our plan didn't pan out, so I had to do what I had to do." A'shai held up the arm that was now wrapped. "The razor was in his mouth. That's some bitch shit. He pulled that shit out quick, too." A'shai was reliving that shit in his head.

"You know we were always trained to expect the unexpected. Thanks for shedding blood for me, bro'." We were in this together, so the blood he shed was a sacrifice so that I wouldn't have, too.

"For sho'." We could talk about all that later. Right

now, it was about getting to the airport before Gavino's flight took off.

With the windows down and the music blasting, before you knew it, we made it to our destination. Gavino gave us strict instructions on what entrance to use. Our guns laid in our laps as we made it closer to the cash payout. I didn't care if I ever saw Gavino again in life or not. I was done with this life. Tonight hit too close to home, and I wasn't in the business of risking lives of people who held a special place. The airport was a ghost town. I guessed Gavino was the only flight out tonight.

We drove on the open black tarmac, looking for a gate F2. After circling a few times, we finally figured it out. In the middle of the tarmac was a Nextant G90XT ready for take-off. There was a flight attendant waiting by the steps of the jet that had two large duffel bags. He was playing the part a little too perfect. There weren't any cars or any indication that there was life on the plane. Why would he be standing there if no one was around? Was Gavino on the plane already and I didn't know it?

A'shai slowed down the car, probably feeling the same way I was feeling.

"This shit don't look off to you?" That was why A'shai was my brother, on the real. The truck came to a complete stop, and we looked at our surroundings.

"You read my mind," I countered.

"What you think we should do? Gavino should be here any minute." I looked at the clock that read 1:45 a.m., which indicated that we were early.

"Something doesn't seem right, bro'. I'm not sure what

it is." I grabbed my Swiss SIG SG 550 assault rifle to go with Ether as the equalizer.

"I'm ready for war." A'shai put the truck in park after checking for his guns.

We got out of the truck and walked around to the trunk to grab the painting. We finally got close enough to the plane that we noticed movement in the cabin.

"You saw that?" I wanted to make sure my eyes weren't playing tricks on me.

"Yup," A'shai agreed.

We didn't even get the chance to guess who it was, before an armed man came out, prompting the other guy to pull out his piece, pointing it our way. We both ran back to the truck, leaving the painting where it was at. We jumped in, and A'shai threw the truck in drive, hitting the automatic window buttons simultaneously before we even had a chance to pull off.

Pop! Pop! Pop!

The back window shattered to pieces. A'shai put his foot to the pedal. We didn't even realize someone creeped up behind us. I looked in the rearview mirror to see another armed assassin. We were so worried about the opps in front of us that we forgot to protect our backs. This was usually a four-part harmony. It didn't matter; we were still getting shit done.

We put our metal to use and opened fire on all three men as we tried to get the hell out of dodge. A'shai was driving, so I had to let my gun speak for the both of us. Before we had a chance to gain traction, our tires were shot out. Tone was a smart motherfucker, but he was going to die tonight.

"Yo, you good?" I asked A'shai. We didn't have time. We had to jump out and kill or be killed.

"Didn't I tell you I was ready for war." A'shai jumped out the truck, bullets flying as the night ate up the excitement in the air.

"Say no more." I jumped out along with him, and we let our guns do the talking for us.

Pop! Pop! Pop!

We took cover behind the truck, allowing them to let off rounds that weren't doing any damage. I looked around, trying to plan our getaway. The truck was sitting on two flats that wasn't going to get us anywhere. We would be exposed if we tried running toward the entrance, so we had no choice but to shoot it out until the last one was standing. They could be calling more people, who knew.

I couldn't believe we got set up.

"This motherfucker set us up." A'shai thought out loud my same thoughts.

"You haven't been hit, right?" I asked, checking myself to make sure. With bullets flying everywhere, I wasn't too sure.

"I'm good. Bro', how we gonna get out of here?" The gunshots had stopped.

Vroom! Vroom!

Skerrt!!

Someone joined us. It probably was Gavino, who had a lot of explaining to do. I peeked over the truck to see if I could get a view without getting my head shot off. A'shai did the same, and when we both noticed who it was, we checked the chamber to make sure we had more bullets. This nigga was going to die today for the part he played in this. How could one be a brother one day and an enemy the next? I stared at Tone while he talked to the other gunman.

"He's mine," A'shai said through a clenched jaw.

"We'll take turns." I needed some time with Tone, too.

"There's nowhere to go. The only way up out of here is in a body bag, brothers," Tone made sure to raise his voice so that we could hear him.

"Fuck you!" A'shai spat back.

"If y'all would have heard me out, we wouldn't be here." Tone cocked his gun and started letting off rounds. "Brothers, come out to playyyyyy." Being cocky would get you killed.

"Don't ever call me your brother!" I shouted.

Pop!

"I was the oldest but yet you got most of the attention. Shit couldn't move without big ol' Mega." His jealousy was felt through his words.

"I don't know what Ruby put in your head, but she was the one who didn't think you were capable." I tried to flip it, which I knew he wasn't buying.

"Guess what? She's going to see that I'm capable now when I bring your head to her on a silver platter."

Pop! Pop!

Tone and his goons were getting closer. I could tell by how close his conversation started to sound. I prepared myself. Someone was going to die tonight, and it wasn't going to be me or A'shai if I could help it. I was really too tired to think of a way out. We didn't have many options. The best option at the moment was to shoot it out and may the best man win. A'shai and I looked at each other, then tapped our guns together.

A'shai mouthed, "Money."

I followed up with, "Power."

He said, "Respect."

I ended with, "Is the key to life."

A'shai started shooting first. Their attention was on him, so I came from the back of the truck and hit one of them. He hit the ground. Bullets rained like the Fourth of July. The way we were shooting, you would have thought we had unlimited ammo. I was able to get that first kill of the night; now it was time for me to get another. I came from around the back of the truck.

Pop! Pop!

I was hit in my right shoulder, which caught me completely off guard. I'd never been shot before. Once A'shai noticed I got shot, he started going crazy.

RAT-A-TAT-A-TAT-A-TAT

One of them on the other side of the truck hit the ground with a thump. Not before another bullet hit me. This time, I wasn't sure where, but I felt something hot. I slid down the side of the truck. A'shai saw me crumble, but he didn't stop shooting, making his way over to me. I was definitely shot by the red stains that were residue on A'shai's hand. He saw that I was still breathing, so he had to finish the job. He acted quickly, opened the back door to the truck, and pulled out another M16.

"Yo, this motherfucker got the painting and the money." I couldn't even stand to see what was going on.

Vroom! Vroom!

"He's fucking getting away." A'shai ran after the car, not letting his finger off the trigger, but Tone was able to get away.

"We gotta get you to the hospital. There's a lot of blood." I never saw panic in A'shai's eyes before. I started to feel a little sleepy and drowsy.

MONA LISA SUTTON

Why couldn't this be a dream? I'd been wondering that all night.

I tossed and turned, wondering if I should call Mega, but I understood that he couldn't stay with me. This was something I had to face on my own. There was an open investigation being done to locate the missing painting. That didn't stop Mr. Michael Weiss from offering me a featured night at the Mets. Gina was going to get with his executive assistant to work out the details. He even invited me to the Met Gala, but I declined. I had to get the gallery in order. I was able to make it to the gallery with two hours of sleep.

"I wish it was a dream, too. This wasn't what Biggie rapped about in his song." Gina was trying to be her genuine self, but she, too, was running on fumes.

"I did some research about the Contini painting, and I

couldn't find much." That was another reason why I didn't get much sleep.

"You know, I did some research of my own. Supposedly, the painter who created the painting won a National Medal of Arts Award, but for some reason, the award was taken away. That was how far I got. The painting was never seen after that."

"Wait, what?" How did Gina find this information? I searched Google, and nothing came up but ads for the pre-fundraiser gala.

"I got skills… and I have software that can track if Bin Laden really died. It even confirmed that Tupac was indeed six feet under."

"Girl, shut up." I laughed, which I never thought I would after the last twenty-four hours.

"Seriously, though. I think our only lead is to find out why the award was taken away. Give me the green light when you are ready to cross that bridge. Who knows what the hell we will uncover."

"Let's see what the investigators for the Mets find, and then we will take it from there." I didn't want to add more stuff on our plate.

"I thought you would be wrapped up in Mega's arms, girl," Gina spoke assuredly.

The movers were here, the employees were wiping down chairs, sweeping, and the floor would be mopped later. I was trying to keep Mega off my mind. I texted him this morning, and he didn't even text me back. I looked for his cars, even the Wraith at the barbershop, and didn't see it. He always parked in the same park. I stressed him out so much that he had to go MIA? This was the part of getting to know someone that I didn't like.

"I thought the same thing, but I haven't heard from him since we left last night." Everything was locked up this morning, so he did keep his word on that.

"That doesn't line up. He's usually on point." Gina was on to something.

"There you go thinking like me again." Gina and I had value points.

"Let me call A'shai." Gina grabbed her phone and called A'shai. His phone went straight to voicemail.

I dialed Mega again for the hell of it, and it went straight to voicemail as well.

"When I called this morning, it wasn't going straight to voicemail." I didn't even know where Mega lived or who his family was. All I knew was this didn't seem like him.

"I'll keep trying A'shai, and you keep trying Mega."

"Okay. I'm going down to the barbershop to see if they heard from him." Gina nodded her head.

Why was all this happening at one time? Hopefully Mega was man enough to say he needed some time to himself. I didn't have time for the games. I had enough going on. I looked out in the parking lot, hoping to see him… hoping that this feeling I had in my gut was wrong. I finally made it to the barbershop, and all three barbers were there. Mega's chair was empty. I had little hope that he was in his office.

"Hey, is Mega here?" I asked Matt the barber.

"No, he hasn't come in yet. I opened the shop. I have

been calling him, but he hasn't gotten back to me yet. Everything okay?"

"When you speak to him, let him know to call me, please."

"I most definitely will." Matt looked like he wanted to ask more questions but didn't want to overstep.

"Thank you." I walked back to the gallery.

"I called Hackensack University Medical Center, and he's there," Gina wasted no time in telling me as I hurried through the doors.

"Wait, huh? What?" I couldn't even form complete sentences.

"Something told me to call the local hospitals. It just so happens Hackensack was the first one since we are right here. I told them I was his sister. They wouldn't give me information over the phone."

"Did they at least say if he was dead or not?" I was hopeful.

"They couldn't."

I stood, staring at Gina, trying to figure out how I ended up in hell.

"Let's go." Gina snatched up the keys and our pocketbooks.

"Gina, stay here. I need this part of my life not to die. Make sure shit gets done so we can get back to our normal lives."

"You sure? I can have one of the staff hold it down," she pleaded.

"Right now, I trust you and only you." For all we knew, it could be one of the staff who drove off with the painting.

"You better call me as soon as you hear something."

"I will." I grabbed my stuff from Gina, gave her a long, much needed hug, and made my way to Hackensack Memorial. It was only eleven minutes away.

My prayers were kind of rusty. I was mad at God for a long time, not understanding why I had to be a motherless child, what I did to deserve a father who only loved me when I fit into his box. Then he sent me two men. One was probably going to hell for his lifestyle, and the other might be dead before I got a chance to know him.

Why couldn't you hide love in the face of death? We fought against the thought of losing someone and never being able to experience that person's presence ever again, that's a scary thing to most people.

The gloomy overcast of the gray skies hovered over my ride as I zipped through the streets. I didn't know if it was going to rain, but it sure matched what I was wearing today. My heart was on my sleeve. The world was about to cry for me, and it couldn't have come at a better time. I needed a cleansing. The sound of rain and thunder cracked the sky. As soon as I pulled up, the rain came down hard. The loud sound of the rain hitting the car exterior created a beat of suspense. It wasn't until I made it into the parking garage that it stopped, bringing me back to the present. I sprinted toward the entrance.

"How can I help you?"

"I'm here to see Mega Dakar." The receptionist took her time keying in his name.

"Mr. Dakar is in the ICU. Only close family is permitted."

"I'm his sister and the only family he has left." I put on my acting hat, and it paid off.

"Go down this hall. The elevators are on your left-hand side. Take it up to the sixth floor. He's in room six-nineteen." I thanked her and did as I was told.

I had a lot of time to prepare myself for what I would say— the car ride over and now the elevator ride up. I held my pocketbook close as I looked for room 619. It was the last door on the hallway. I knocked before entering, but no one was there except a body laying in the bed. My hand covered my mouth at all the machines that Mega was hooked up to. He didn't have any bruises on his face. It didn't look like he was in a bad accident. The machines looked to be breathing for him though. My eyes were getting watery.

"Mega, can you hear me?" My hands glided across his body, being sure not to hurt him.

Silence...

I wished I could kiss his lips, but it was impossible in his condition. I settled for a kiss on his forehead. I wondered where A'shai was. Was he hurt, too? You rarely saw one without the other, unless Mega was working. Did Mega get attacked while he was closing up the gallery? He never texted me that he made it home last night. I sat down next to his bed, baffled, replaying the whole night in my head.

"What happened, Mega?" I asked earnestly.

Beep. Beep. Beep

The beeping from the machines was the only answer I got.

"I think I love you." I gripped Mega's huge hands in mine.

The machines started going crazy, beeping like a time bomb was going off. I hurried to call the nurse.

"Somebody, help me!" I screamed out in the hallway.

"Ma'am, we are going to have to ask you to step out." The nurses and doctors came rushing in.

I couldn't move.

"Ma'am, please. We need you to move." One of the staff moved me out into the hallway as they worked on Mega. I cried like the rain tapping the windowpane.

"Mona." I looked up at someone calling my name. It was A'shai.

I ran to him, balling my eyes out. His arm was bandaged up, and he had blood all over his clothes.

"They kicked me out to work on him," I was able to get out between sobs.

"My brother is a fighter; don't worry about it." I wished I had the same energy A'shai did.

A'shai walked past me to the room, and the doctors and nurses were coming back out.

"Are you kin to Mr. Dakar?" The doctor approached A'shai.

I was imagining the worst.

MEGA DAKAR

BEEP. *Beep. Beep.*

"How long are you going to continue to act like you don't know nothing?"

I heard low voices in between the beeping of a machine. I couldn't move. I felt like I was dreaming but I was awake.

"I'm not the person you should be asking. I already told you that."

Their voices started to become familiar as I started to push myself to open my eyes. I had cottonmouth, which made it hard for me to swallow. The brightness of the lights had me thinking this was the end. It wasn't until my eyes focused that I noticed where I was. I looked straight ahead at the TV playing a rerun of Moesha. I was successful in turning my head to the left, seeing Mona jump to her feet.

"He's awake, A'shai. He's awake." Mona grabbed me and rubbed my face.

"I got eyes, just like you got eyes." A'shai looked on.

If I had strength to laugh, this would have been the moment. I was hooked up to a monitor and an IV.

"What happened?" Mona asked, concerned.

"Can we make sure he can talk first before you start interrogating him?" A'shai was bandaged which brought me back to why I was here. "As a matter of fact, can you give us a few moments to discuss something?"

Someone walked in, and we all looked toward the door to see who it was.

"Mr. Dakar, I see you are up. My name is Nurse Dotti, and I want to check some of your vitals. By the looks of it, you're doing good." Nurse Dotti did what nurses do, but you could tell Mona and A'shai wanted to get back to their exchange. "Everything looks good. Dr. Patel will be in a little later on. Today is his late day." Nurse Dotti wrote something on a board and was on her way.

"Y'all gonna tell me what happened. I'm owed that. I need to know if my life is in danger. All this shit ain't a coincidence. People just don't get shot for nothing. So spill it," Mona spat as soon as the door closed.

"She… she can…" I cleared my throat. Mona poured me some water, and I drank some out of the straw. "She can stay." It was a little raspy, but I was sure they heard me.

"You sure about that? I just want to make sure you coherent and shit."

I knew this meant that I would have to come clean. I shook my head yes.

"I think we got set up." A'shai told me something I already knew. It was no way I would be laying up in this hospital bed if that wasn't the case. I looked at Mona as she held onto every word.

"The two cats that were with Tone had to be Gavino's people. How else would they get access to his plane?" Ruby wouldn't go against Gavino just to get back at me.

"That's two people I gotta handle: Ruby Rose and Gavino Contini. How you trying to handle this?" This part of the conversation would need to wait until we were alone.

"Wait, Contini? Does this have anything to do with the Maurizio Contini painting?" Tears formed in Mona's eyes without me answering the question.

"Take a seat for me, Mo Love."

"No, I'll stand." Mona pulled away from me, crossing her arms.

"I haven't been completely honest with you about what I do for a living." I took a pause to see if she was going to say anything, but she didn't. "Not only do I own the barbershop, but I do contract work for some very powerful people."

"Okay, you got a side hustle. Do these powerful people make you do illegal stuff?" Mona questioned.

I looked over at A'shai who shook his head.

"Nobody makes me do nothing. We provide a service and get paid for it."

"Just answer the question. All I need is a yes or no." Mona stood firm in wanting an answer.

"Yes." I couldn't say much after that.

"Get to the part where you tell me how I play a part in all of this?" You could hear the frustration in Mona's voice.

"Before I met you, we were asked to do a job for an Italian dude named Gavino Contini. We had done some work for him back in the day when we were just making a name for ourselves. Just like with that contract, we were set to make a lot of money to get him what he wanted. Unfortunately, he wanted something that was at Picturesque that he claimed was a family heirloom." I knew that last part would hurt her.

"So, you mean to tell me, you were the one who stole the painting?"

"No, I did." A'shai spoke up, always willing to show up for me.

Mona looked at A'shai like he'd lost his mind.

"I'm sorry, Mona. Me and you already had… gotten close before I knew what the job entailed." I wanted to say we already had fallen in love, but I didn't want her to think I was only saying it because I got caught.

"The whole night… the whole night you laughed with me, kissed me, and acted like nothing was wrong. All along, you were plotting to take from me. You jeopardized my career, all for what? Money. Yes, you knew about the job before you met me, but obviously, I wasn't good enough for you to change your mind."

"That's not the type of people we deal with," I let her know.

"Oh, big ol' Mega is scared to choose what's right because doing wrong is so much easier. I told you not to break my heart, and you couldn't help yourself." Mona snatched up what she came with and was out the door before I had a chance to say anything.

A'shai and I sat in silence for a few minutes.

"I need you to keep an eye on her until I get out of the hospital."

"No doubt."

"The only good thing about me laying in this hospital bed, it gives me time to think." It was uncomfortable as hell, but it slowed me down enough to plan.

"Aight, yo. I'm out. I'm going to let you get some rest, and hopefully they can discharge you within the next few days."

"I hope so. We got work to do." A'shai gave me a pound and was out the door.

I looked at the hospital ceiling, wishing I wasn't in the predicament I was in. It was always a possibility that Mona would find out, and I thought I did everything in my power to protect her. It was when you didn't have everyone playing on the same team that things went left. Something was off about the job since day one, so that was why I had to switch up our original plan.

The door opened, and I thought I had seen a ghost.

She still looked the same but a little older. Their features were almost identical.

"You didn't really think Gavino wouldn't know the painting was a fake?"

How in the hell?

"From one artist to the next, you gotta pay attention to detail if you want to duplicate a painting."

"I don't know what you are talking about." I tried to play it off.

She made her way over to my bed and snatched the nurse call button and tied my hands to the bed. She put tape over my mouth. I tried like hell to get out the restraints and must have busted open one of my wounds. Red was staining the white sheets. I couldn't move. I couldn't yell... all I could do was listen. She pulled up a seat and got comfortable while pain shot through my body from the fight to be free.

"See, what you didn't realize is that every canvas is different. You didn't create your fake on a museo linen canvas. The cotton canvas you used was a dead giveaway. How dare you insult my intelligence!" She snatched the tape off my mouth. "If you yell, you will be dead before anybody makes it in here."

Yelling was an option, but I wasn't going out like that.

"You're delusional, just like your husband," I said to her.

Gavino's wife, Geneva, was sent to finish me off gangsta style. Instead of doing it himself, he sent a woman to do his dirty work. A part of me wanted to start yelling, but if I was going to go out, I was going to go out with my pride. I had one up on her though. I still knew where the original painting was. I was sure Gavino still wanted it, or he would have lost out on the $250,000 he gave us.

"That painting represented sacrifice. Our family's blood was shed for a painting that I thought would change my life forever."

"Your life?" This sounded personal.

"All I ever wanted to do was be a famous painter. I didn't have a dick between my legs, so that dream never quite manifested. So I had to show them that there were ways around that." Geneva nodded her head, thinking back on that time.

"Show them what?" I was so confused.

"I am Maurizio Contini, the painter," Geneva shared like it wasn't a big deal.

"So you just chose a random name to become famous?" There were still a lot of things that didn't make sense.

"Maurizio Contini was my son's name until they killed him."

"Who killed him?" I was trying to buy time, hoping that a nurse or doctor would walk in.

"The powers that be, they not only stripped me of my Medal of Arts, but they killed my son in the process. I'll do anything to bring him back. Fame wasn't worth his life."

It all made sense now. The painting was a low-key sacrifice. It was a reminder that the Contini family lost a part of them. Geneva was chasing fame, and it backfired on her. It was like she traded one for the other, only to still be left with nothing. I didn't know if I would even want that reminder staring me in my face, so I wasn't sure why the Contini family wanted it back.

"When I created that painting, that was the happiest I had ever been, in a really long time. Things started to look up until it was time for me to receive the Medal of Arts. My first painting under my alias was being talked about. It even sold for almost seven million dollars."

"How did you get caught?" I was interested, but I also was trying to get off task.

"Someone I once loved called and reported me." That seemed to anger her, snapping her back from traveling down memory lane.

"You really don't have to do this." I hoped I sounded convincing.

"You should have done what you were told." Geneva pulled out a syringe filled with clear liquid. I squirmed in the bed, and she quickly put the tape back over my mouth.

The door swung open. *Saved by the bell.*

"Mega, I gotta get this shit off my—" Mona stopped in her tracks. She didn't realize at first that it wasn't just me in the room. The syringe dropped out of Geneva's hand and hit the floor as her mouth hung wide open. I looked back and forth between Mona and Geneva as they continued to look at each other. I knew my eyes weren't playing tricks on me. They looked like twins.

"You're alive?" Mona asked, trying to understand as I had earlier.

MONA LISA SUTTON

THIS HAD TO BE A DREAM. That was the only time I was able to see and spend time with the woman who gave birth to me. She looked just how I imagined after all these years. The way my dad talked about her you would have thought she was a devil in disguise. She was real and breathing. Why was she there in the hospital room with Mega? Was it something else he wasn't telling me? I stood frozen, not knowing what to do.

"Mona Lisa Stutton, you are as beautiful as I can remember." The lady's tears replaced the stare down. I didn't know what to call or label her. She came closer to me, reaching in for a hug.

"Please, don't touch me. I haven't seen you in almost thirty years, and you want to act like nothing happened." I pushed her from me.

"Baby, I—"

"I'm not your baby. Babies don't get left for dead by a parent who they are supposed to do life with."

"It was way more complicated than that, Mona." I didn't know why my rejection got her a little irritated.

"You damn right it is. You not being in my life, made my life complicated. How could you leave your five-year-old child with a man who was bitter?"

"Your father was a great man. He just didn't have the same zeal that I did. He was okay with working a nine to five on a teacher's salary. I wanted more; I needed more. I was going to come back for you," she pleaded.

"The last time I looked up the word was, it was considered past tense. In this case, it meant that it never took place. So don't tell me you was. Tell me why you didn't." Everything else didn't matter.

"When I left to study abroad, your father was so angry that he forbade me to see you. I guess as leverage for me not to go. At first, I thought he was bluffing, but after a few missed phone calls and unanswered letters, I stopped trying." She took a pause, trying to layer the story. "I had grown to love Italy for all the opportunities that it afforded me, so I wanted to stay but bring you with me. I flew home to come get you, but your father made it clear that I couldn't leave with you."

"I would have remembered you coming back. There were many nights I stayed awake waiting for you to tuck me in. Those nights never came."

"You were at school, sweetheart, and by the time you

got out, Kurt had already scared me off. I never saw him so mad, so much so that he sent me home with a bruised face. Kurt had never put his hands on me before. When I wouldn't sleep with him, he felt like I was cheating on him in Italy, which I wasn't. I just didn't like the way he was treating me."

"Daddy said you left us for a guy. Where he at?" I looked around the room, being a smart ass.

"I didn't leave you guys for Gavino. Your dad ran me off, and I didn't have it in me to fight, so I went back to Italy, and that's when I met my husband."

Gavino was who Mega and A'shai were talking about earlier.

"You knew about this?" I questioned Mega. He was striking out today. He wasn't who I thought he was. I was giving my time and attention to someone who I truly didn't know.

"He's innocent. The only thing he is guilty of is not completing what he was paid to do." Geneva kneeled, picking up something that she turned her back to conceal.

"I wasn't paid to do shit. I hope killing me is worth it." There was no remorse in Mega's words, causing me to realize what Geneva was sent here to do.

"What... What you mean... kill... you were 'bout to kill him?" I rushed over to where she was standing.

"Mona, some very powerful people want him dead. I must admit, Mega, you are a smart man. You must really love her if you took time to duplicate such a complex painting." I wasn't sure what Geneva was talking about.

"Duplicate? What painting?" There were a lot of pieces to this puzzle, I see. I looked between Mega and Geneva to see which one was going to tell me what was going on.

"I did what I had to do, but I still protected you. I was too deep in it with you to totally crush your heart. I made my own version of the Maurizio Contini painting and kept the original as insurance. I'm glad I did, too. A'shai and I were set up to be killed, and we weren't going out like that."

"Mega, please just give them the painting." Who cared at this point. I would rather have him alive.

"I think you need to listen to your girlfriend, for all of our sakes."

"I know how the game works, Geneva. Even if I give you the painting, your husband is still going to come for my life." Mega had a point.

"If he gives you the painting, you have to promise me that he'll be left alone. You at least owe me that... Mother." I never asked her for anything, and I never would.

"You don't have to do that, Mo Love," Mega stated. I went from hating Mega to admiring how, even when his back was up against the wall, he had me in mind. Geneva broke down crying out of nowhere, scaring the hell out of me. Mega and I looked at each other. I was watching her to see if this was another one of her games.

"You called her Mo Love. That is so cute. Why couldn't your father love me like that?" I looked at Geneva like how the hell would I know. She continued. "All I wanted your father to do was support my dreams and love me while doing it. His stuff, his career was always more important than mine. I just wish you didn't get caught up in our mess."

Me and her both had something in common.

"Do we have a deal?" All the rest of what she was saying could wait. That wait was predicated on if we could trust her or not.

"Deal," she said through sobs, trying to get herself together.

"How we know if we can trust you?" Mega read my mind. Geneva thought about it for a minute.

"Gavino wasn't the only person behind your death sentence. Ruby is the one that ordered the hit. Gavino only needed your services to get the painting. Ruby worked out a deal to have you wiped out. That's how you know you can trust me," Geneva spilled to seal the deal.

"Say no more." Mega was on his phone with the quickness.

"I'll be in touch." Geneva looked my way, hesitating before walking out with her head down.

I collapsed on the chair once the door closed. I felt like I hadn't been breathing, like I was holding my breath the whole time in Geneva's presence. She still had a hold on me; my love for her was lying dormant. This was a weird way to meet the women who gave birth to me. I caught her about to kill the man I was in love with for the guy she left my dad for. I couldn't wait to tell Gina about this shit.

It didn't take A'shai too long to get to the hospital. He was busting through the doors.

"Ruby put a tag on our head. Gavino was only

benefiting from it. Ruby and Tone validated. I'll bring you up to speed about Gavino at another time."

"Don't worry. I'll handle that tonight."

"Money," A'shai proudly spoke.

"Power." Mega radiated it, even in his down state.

"Respect," A'shai demanded.

"Is the key to life," Mega ended off with.

MONA LISA SUTTON

"You need to write a book about your life. This some Jerry Springer shit," Gina said, helping me prepare for what I had to do.

"Girl, tell me about it. This whole weekend has been one thing after another. I can't keep up." I was mentally exhausted.

"Are you at least happy that your mother is still alive, and you got to see her?" Gina's question was something that I'd been going back and forth about.

"I almost saw her kill, Mega. That was my first impression of her. We both know that first impressions matter. I can't get that out of my head."

"You better than me. I would have whupped her ass before and after I found out she was my momma." Gina and I laughed. I wouldn't put it past Gina. I'd seen and heard of her doing some crazy things.

"Don't tempt me. I still have time," I let be known.

Geneva was on her way to get the original Maurizio Contini painting in exchange for Mega's life. I was scared that something was going to go down that I wouldn't have control over. That was why Gina was here, to make sure everything went as planned. I looked at the painting, tracing every area of the canvas, seeing it up close for the first time. The pictures didn't do it any justice. Was it worth all the hype it was getting? No, but it was a unique painting which was why it was highly sought after. Geneva and Gavino could have it. I wanted to move on with my life.

"I'm going to help you with the painting to the back door. I'll wait until your m— I mean Geneva comes, hopefully you can get some shit off your chest." We both grabbed the painting, taking it to the back. Instructions were given to Geneva to come to the back of the gallery. We waited for about fifteen minutes for her to arrive. Before you knew it, Geneva and I were face to face.

"Mona, let me know if I need to slide a bitch. I'm still on the committee, and I'm below my quote for the year." Gina stared at Geneva, giving me a hug before walking back into the gallery.

"You need to tell your little friend I don't take kindly to threats." Geneva had a dark side to her, and that was the person I got to meet.

"I'm not telling her anything. It's good to have somebody to have your back. Gina has been there for me since I can remember. What I also remember is, you weren't." I gave Geneva a now what look.

"I get it, you hate me, but you'll see as a parent that

every choice you make won't be the right one. We all are human, and mothers make mistakes, too." Geneva could miss me with all that. Nothing excuses the trauma that was placed on my life.

"You should hate yourself. You failed me, and the way you are talking is like I'm just supposed to forgive. Nah, it doesn't work like that. This is years of built-up anger that I had to release. Why not release it on the person who caused it? Riddle me that."

"I lost two kids in this lifetime, so I know I failed. I'm not asking you to forgive me. I'm asking for you to understand my side. That's all."

"Two kids?" How dare she have another baby and not take care of the first one she gave birth to. I shook my head at the irony.

"Your brother's name was Maurizio, but he was murdered by the Italian Mafia who brought this painting almost twenty-eight years ago. Maurizio never got a chance to live. He wasn't even two before they shot up our house and killed him," Gina said, looking at the painting. Her eyes were filled with water as she tried to hold it in.

To know I had a brother was a slap in my face. How could she lay down and make another baby? I hoped Maurizio was resting in peace. At least he got peace while I had to deal with rejection, isolation, and depression all my life. To me, he got the easy way out. I lived a life that I didn't choose, and the absence of this lady standing before me proved that. I always had in my mind how I wanted my life to be but never had the courage to change it. It wasn't until recently that I decided it was time for me to have that life. This was a new beginning, and I couldn't be happier to turn this page and start a new chapter.

"How's your father doing?" Geneva had a lot of got damn nerve asking about my dad.

"Wouldn't you want to know. None of your business." I rolled my eyes at her boldness.

"I was asking because I really want to get to know you, Mona, and this time, I didn't want Kurt to get in the way of that."

"Oh, so you think helping Mega creates an open door to building a relationship with me?" She must have lost her ever loving mind.

"All I can do is hope that one day you will change your mind. I told you my part of the story. Talk to your father so he can tell you the hand he played in it. It's not all on me, baby." Geneva did have a point. I hadn't spoken to my dad yet because of everything that'd been going on, but we were definitely going to have a conversation.

"If you keep your word about keeping Gavino from killing Mega, I'll think about it." It was some truth in that.

"Gavino doesn't want me to leave him, so he'll do anything I say, so Mega is safe." I was relieved. "I'm glad you were able to experience the love you have with Mega. It reminds me of me and your dad in our early days. That love is incomparable; it's a love that people only read and dream about." I didn't know how Geneva put those two pieces of the puzzle together, but I hoped she was right.

"Everybody I love seems to leave me or break my heart in a way that it was almost impossible to put it back together. How can I trust when everybody I encounter is not trustworthy?" I was thinking out loud.

"Honey, listen. Love is built on the different obstacles you face. Most people give up during the building stage because they are scared to lose themselves. Mona, get lost in every moment you have with the people you love, even when they seem unlovable. Or you end up like me, with so many regrets." Geneva looked at me once more, grabbed up the painting, and made her way out the door.

I didn't know if I'd ever see her again. As of right now, I didn't care if I did. I had to get back on track, so I was checking all negativity at the door. It was my turn to be happy, by any means necessary. I got a lot of closure within these past couple of weeks. First my dad opened up, then Tyrell apologized, and finding out about my mother was taxing but needed. I didn't know what this next season would hold. I did know who I wanted with me as I navigated this next chapter.

"You got some nice booty cheeks." I couldn't help but laugh at Mega trying to cover up his backside from the exposure of his hospital gown.

"I shoot people for less; you better stop playing with me." I stopped laughing because that wasn't funny. Mega had a huge smile on his face though.

"Don't play like that," I said sternly.

"It was a joke," Mega said, laughing.

"I see someone is in good spirits. You even starting to

look like yourself." I watched on, admiring the perfection before me, even in his hospital gown.

"I'm being discharged today. They actually told me to get dressed, which I was doing before you walked in trying to squeeze my butt." Mega was over exaggerating.

"I know you're happy," I said, being well aware that hospitals were the worst.

"I'm happy to be able to get out of here so I can hold you, kiss you, and sex you without being interrupted. Although you've been here every day since you found out, despite knowing what happened. That made me love you more." Mega left me speechless.

"Are you sure about that love thing?" Out of everything he said, that was what I chose to focus on.

"Yes, Mo Love. I love you. Not only because you held me down. I love you because you are an amazing individual who also happens to be drop dead gorgeous. Why do you think I almost died?" Again, Mega was not funny with the last statement.

"You almost died being stupid." I chuckled at that. "I don't know too much about this love thing, but I love you, too, Mega. At least I think I do."

"I'm willing to take that chance so you can learn what real love is. Mona Lisa Sutton, will you be my girl?" Mega got down on one knee.

"Yes, Mega, I will." I didn't have to think about it. I already knew what I wanted. I was glad he wanted the same thing.

MEGA DAKAR

LIFE GOT REAL when you had a machine breathing for you; it was like a wakeup call you didn't know you needed. You couldn't keep a good man down if you tried. I was a few weeks post operation, and the weights I was lifting in the gym were telling a different story. Having to count on people to help you eat, take a piss, and shit was something I would never want to experience again, which made me workout harder, day in and day out, to get to the healthiest I'd ever been. My wounds were healing, but mentally, the only way for me to move on was to see both Ruby and Tone take their last breaths.

Ruby had a lot of connections that could make her disappear, so I was sure she called in a favor to do just that. We were going to catch up with her one way or another, but it wasn't happening quick enough. We put a bounty on their heads, and we had people willing to make the money, but they hadn't shown their faces yet.

"I'm just as frustrated as you are."

A'shai spotted me on the bench press. My right shoulder was hit, but I was getting my strength back. I wasn't lifting what I normally would, but it was doing the job.

"The city was swept clean; there weren't any traces of either of them. At this point, they could be anywhere." I think that was what bothered me the most. We checked off every name on the list of places they could be. We even talked with a few past clients who hadn't heard from Ruby.

"How long it takes us to find them doesn't matter. I'm going to make them suffer just as long."

My set was done, so I got up and let A'shai get in position to let off some steam.

"They tried to play God when it came to my life, and that's unforgivable, so it's not over. There is always a way; we just haven't found it yet." I looked on as A'shai knocked out his set.

I wanted to enter my new life without having to look over my shoulder forever. I wanted to be able to sleep at night, knowing I made the right decision to leave the jungle of the streets. I wasn't sure if it was even possible. I was going to do whatever it took to find out if it was. This was a loose end that should have been tied up almost two months ago. It did allow me some time to get ready for battle. We knew it wasn't going to be easy, but now the clock was ticking.

"Has Mona asked anything else about what went down?"

We took a minute to relax before ending our workout with some pushups.

"She hasn't said anything to me about it, but I don't think it settled with her yet. At times, I feel like she's past it, but us shaking down the city isn't helping. Once we move past all this, I can explain it to her so we can move on. Right now, my main focus is to subtract two from the US Census." I got in position on the floor to knock out my hundred pushups.

"Why your phone keeps going off?" A'shai asked as he got down to do his hundred.

"It's this weird number that has been calling me since this morning. I haven't really had time to check on it." If this wasn't my personal phone, I would have answered it. Not too many people had the privilege of having my direct line. "I tried calling it back on the burner, but it won't ring." The call finally went to voicemail, and I waited to see if they would leave a message.

"Next time they call, answer it. Shit, you never know."

A'shai's point had me thinking; Ruby did know my personal number.

My phone buzzed again, this time with a text message.

+3675639526:
Answer

A'shai and I both looked at each other, seeing the message with thoughts of who was behind it.

"They better have something to say that would explain why they've been calling my phone off the hook." Something told me that it wasn't personal, so inserting themselves in my personal space was a violation.

"This might be what we been waiting on, so whatever you do, don't miss that next call."

We gathered our things, ready to make our exit.

"I got this, don't worry. I want them just as bad as you do. I still can't believe we are hunting down people we broke bread with. We only do that with family, the people we love and the people we trust. That shit doesn't sit on your brain?" I looked A'shai's way for his answer as we walked toward our cars.

"I keep playing back times where it could have gone wrong. It was like, one day, we were all good, and then the next day, we were letting our guns do the talking. That shit weird. Our heads must have been in the clouds to have missed the warning signs of when things started changing."

A'shai shook his head just as perplexed as I was.

"We both weren't the same after Mya died. We had other shit on our mind. They weren't as close to her as we were, so in a way, it has always been divided. When Star and Tone stayed home after we left, that showed me they needed Ruby a lot more than we did." They were weak and couldn't make decisions on their own. They were easy targets for her mind games.

"I think the difference is they were looking for a mother, we were looking for a come up. I remember the first time you took me to Ruby's house. She fed us, let us watch her big TV, and gave us somewhere comfortable to sleep. She had me the first night without even hearing her proposition. I just didn't want to have to go back to the group home or an abandoned house."

A'shai didn't talk about his childhood much, but I knew he still got reminders of the past.

"Based off what we know now, was it all worth it?" Regret only made living in vain when looking at it from a negative viewpoint. Who knows if we would have survived without Ruby. That was one of those what ifs that constantly reared its ugly head in situations like this.

"For me it was... I wasn't supposed to make it, bro'. I should either be dead, strung out, or in jail if I followed in the footsteps of the ones before me. Ruby gave me a chance, even if it was for her gain, I gained a lot, too."

A'shai wasn't lying, all he was spittin' was facts.

"All those things she taught us are going to bite her in the ass when we catch up with her. I promise you that." We dapped each other up then got in our whips.

Buzz, buzz, buzz

My phone was ringing, and that crazy number popped up. I blew the horn to signal A'shai before he pulled off. I answered on speaker.

"Hello, who's this?" I said just as A'shai got in the passenger seat.

"I'm glad you decided to answer, son-in-law."

At first, I didn't catch the voice until the end of her statement.

"Geneva?" I asked to confirm what I already knew. A'shai was listening intently.

"Yes, this is she. You better be over there treating my daughter well."

"I think I'm doing a lot better than you ever did." I knew she wasn't calling for this bullshit; she'd better spit it out.

"Listen, I have something you want, so you better play nice, or you'll never get the revenge you so desperately need."

It was like Geneva was mocking me through the phone. Her voice went from soft to conniving in seconds.

"Is that right? I'm supposed to trust you?" It had to be more to what she was letting on, so I wanted her to continue.

"You don't have a choice. If I don't give you this information, you'll never find who you are looking for."

A'shai and I both looked at each other.

"How much will it cost us to get this information?" I knew her asking price would be higher than the original bounty fee.

"I want a meeting with my daughter and her father."

I could make a lot of stuff happen, but I didn't think that was possible.

"I don't want to bring Mona in this. She has already been through enough." It would be like reopening wounds that hadn't completely healed.

"The only way to give you what you want, you have to give me what I want. I don't need the money; I need my daughter to know the complicated truth."

Geneva's voice cracked a little without her permission as she made her request known.

"Why now? You went years without explaining yourself or your side of the story. What's different?" These were questions that needed answers before I shook Mona's foundation again.

"Out of sight, out of mind is how I dealt with what I did. It wasn't until I got to see Mona's face that I realized how detached I was from motherhood. Even through her anger, I still felt a connection that only we could share."

Geneva paused, then continued. "I also want to show her father that he didn't break me. He may have turned my daughter against me, but there's still time to redeem myself, and what better time than now," Geneva concluded.

"I'll see what I can do. It's no guarantee that I can get Mona to agree to what you're asking, but I'll try."

"I don't need you to try. Just do it. I'll be calling you around ten o'clock tonight to confirm. Once we have everything mapped out, then we can talk about everything else."

The phone line went dead.

"Yo, what the hell was that about?"

A'shai spoke right away after we realized the phone was disconnected.

"She didn't even tell us that she had them. She only insinuated that she had what we want. We have to play this right, especially if she wasn't bluffing. Give me a few hours to figure this shit out."

"While you do some figuring out, I'll be doing the same." A'shai paused before continuing.

"Money."

"Power," I followed up.

"Respect," A'shai echoed.

"Is the key to life," I finished.

We went our separate ways, with a lot to think about. Geneva didn't say much but said a lot all at the same time. I didn't know how I would break the news to Mona. All I knew was I had to do it. There probably was a short window of opportunity to capture Ruby and Tone, so I had to calculate each step precisely.

Before I pulled off, I shot a quick text to Mona.

> Meet me at my house for dinner at seven p.m.

If I didn't let Mona know ahead of time, she'd be walking in way past ten p.m., and that wouldn't help an already time sensitive matter.

Dinner was delivered, and on the table, ready for Mona when she pulled up. I couldn't concentrate enough to make our meals, but Chef Travis came through. I'd been preparing for this conversation all day, knowing damn well that was not how I moved. I didn't care if Mona was late, as long as she was here for me to get an answer. I had about an hour and a half to persuade her that all of this was a good idea.

"What's going on, Mo Love." I met her at the door with a glass of something smooth that I made just for her. I kissed her lips, grabbed her pocketbook out her hand, and replaced it with some Henny Sangria. The summer vibes glistened with Mona's skin as it adjusted to the central air condition. The heat wave had her showing more skin than I was used to.

"I'm sorry I'm late. I took a last-minute meeting that went longer than it should have."

Mona kicked off her heels and made her way to the kitchen. I put her purse in the room and joined her.

"You cooked this?"

Mona sipped from her glass and smiled. We were having grilled chicken breasts topped with creamy parmesan and garlic cheese crust and a loaded baked potato.

"Not this time, but I got you. I ain't no chef or nothing, but I can make something taste good." I made sure Mona was comfortable before taking my seat with her at the table.

"I wonder what I gotta do for you to cook for me, if it's like that."

Mona winked, and we both let out a light laugh. I could tell she was tired from how low her eyes were and from the sigh that escaped her, in the few minutes we talked.

"I'll do anything for you. All you have to do is just ask." The past two months, Mona showed up for me in ways that only a few had done.

"Do you ever think you could be completely honest with me about who you really are?"

Mona started prepping her food to eat by cutting into her chicken.

"You know who I am. I'm the same person who told you I loved you, and I meant it." I really did believe Mona was my second chance at love.

"Will your past always interfere with our happiness?"

The way she asked it with no hope was what caught my attention. I didn't know if it was her woman's intuition or not, but I heard her loud and clear.

"Who knows, honestly. I've done enough in this lifetime to have karma come around ten times. I've also only done what I could do with the foundation given to me from conception. Is who I am too much for you?" Her answer would determine the next course of action.

"The problem is you are still hiding stuff like I'm dumb and naïve, Mega. My guess is you are trying to get back at the people who tried to kill you… Just say that. Do I agree or approve of your way of thinking…? No, but you are going to do what you are going to do. All I'm asking is for you to open up to me just a little so I'm not blindsided."

There was a lot of passion in Mona's voice.

"You are absolutely correct. So, here it is… I can't live freely if they are still breathing. I know these people; they won't stop until I'm nailed to the cross and… I need your help."

This was something I knew Mona didn't see coming. I never had to ask for help before from anybody. This was what my life had become, and I guessed I wouldn't see the lessons until this was all over. I learned a lot about myself this past year that I only explored after loss. It took me a minute to embrace it, but I'd been adjusting not only for me but for Mona and our relationship. During my recovery, I discovered I could count on her to remind me how important it was to just inhale and exhale.

"You need help with what?"

Mona's eyes hounded me.

"Today I got a call from someone that knows the whereabouts of the two people who tried to kill me. The only way they will help me is if you talk with them." Mona looked very confused.

"What they want with me?"

There was attitude behind every syllable.

"Ruby, my foster mother, and someone who I called my brother have it out for me. We are still trying to figure out why, and the only one who can answer that is them. When Mya died, things started going left with all of us. A'shai and I no longer lived at the house, but Tone and Star did, so who knows what went on behind closed doors. The day I met you was the day we buried Star and the day I promised to leave this life. We had one more job lined up, which happened to be for the Maurizio Contini painting. All the while, we were being set up by Ruby to be taken out by the Italians." I paused to let it all sink in.

"Your mother called me, and in exchange for Ruby and Tone's whereabouts, she wants to meet with you and your father." Mona's eyes grew darker by the tail end of what this was all about.

"You talked to Geneva?"

Mona couldn't believe what she was hearing.

"Yes. Somehow, she got my number and called this morning, wanting to plead her case to you."

"You see, you see... this is what I mean. Why can't your past leave my past where it's at? Huh? I wanted to believe that life goes on, but something told me that this wasn't over. Why are your demons teaming up with my demons?"

Tears started erupting from Mona's eyes. I reached for her, but she backed away.

"I wish I had all the answers, but I don't. This is closure for both of us. You always wondered what happened, and now this is your chance to finally find out the truth. Both your mother and your father had different stories, so why not hear both of them at the same time? I do need you to do this for me, but it's about you, too, Mo Love."

"You are damn right it's about me, and I have to be honest with myself. After seeing Geneva, hearing her voice brought me back to the golden days of my childhood. She was familiar, but yet a stranger to who I was becoming, in spite of her doing."

Mona chuckled while letting the tears journey down her face.

"So, yeah… this closure is for me, but let me say this. No more secrets, and you have to learn to communicate, even when it's outside of my understanding. I get you had a life before me; it's time to protect the life you have now."

Mona grabbed the napkin and wiped her face the best she could.

"That's my goal. I promise you that." This time when I leaned in and grabbed her hand, she didn't back away. She even allowed me to kiss her lips, three times for I love you.

"What's the plan?" Mona asked, ready to take on what lay ahead.

"You sure you are ready for this?" I wanted to make

sure before I got down to it. I looked for signs of apprehension, but I didn't see any.

"I've been preparing for this my whole life; you have no idea. I just want you to be safe, alive, and not in jail for the part you play."

Mona didn't have to worry. My new life gave me the ambition to eliminate those worries. I laid my hand on my heart as a sign that I had this, thanking her for caring all at the same time.

"Geneva will be calling around ten p.m. to confirm that you agreed to meet with her. Do you think you will be able to get your father to agree?" That was a part of it that I had no clue about.

"The only way is to show up at his house. I have a key, but last I checked, his baby momma was staying with him. That's sure to cause a lot of problems."

Mona was in deep thought, weighing the pros and cons of her first thought.

"If your father is licensed to carry, I don't think that's a great idea. I really don't want to get the cops involved; we will have the Italians all over our ass." Mona's dad was a key player for both of us.

"I don't think it would get there. If it gets that bad, we can leave, and Geneva would have to just deal with it. Mr. Kurt Sutton does what he wants and doesn't care who it affects in its aftermath; if anybody knows, it's her."

That sounded just like the man I met.

"What's plan B if that doesn't work? You gotta always have a backup plan."

"I'm not jumping through hoops for Geneva. She doesn't need my father to make herself heard. We did what she asked—we set up the meeting. It's not our fault if it's not received well."

Mona shrugged her shoulders.

We talked for a little more, both trying to imagine the outcome of our dilemma. The food got cold because we had no appetite. We literally sat around, waiting for Geneva's call to put all that we spoke about into action. I kept stealing glances at Mona to make sure she was in a fit state to go through with it. Other than her fighting her sleepiness, she seemed okay to me. This was a lot to take in, so I would understand if her mood wasn't inviting. My phone vibrated with a text message.

> +3675639526:
>
> I hope you are going to tell me something I want to hear. Pickup in 5 minutes.

It was a text from Geneva. Mona's eyes grew big after I showed her the message, but she stayed calm. It was the longest five minutes of our lives, waiting for this call.

Buzz, buzz, buzz

"Hello." I quickly put it on speaker for Mona to hear.

"Do we have an agreement or not?"

Geneva got right down to it.

"It depends on if you have what I want or not," I countered.

"Didn't I tell you I'll deliver if you delivered? Listen, I have something you want, and you have something I want.

Either you're going to give it to me, or this conversation is for nothing."

Geneva's words were stone cold.

"What you mean he has something you want? This isn't a bid to the highest buyer. This is my life that you keep playing with." Mona couldn't contain herself. "The only reason I'm agreeing to this is so I can move on with my life. Haven't you done enough damage, Geneva?"

Mona threw her hands in the air and was shaking her head as if Geneva could see her distressed.

"Mona, I… I really wish this never happened to our family, but it did. I need you to hear both sides of our story."

Geneva's voice softened a little, taking a different approach on how she dealt with her daughter.

"I don't think anything either of you tell me will make me see things differently. Honestly, let's get it over with." Mona sighed.

"Geneva, how we going to do this?" I moved the conversation along.

"I'll have both Ruby and Tone to you by the close of business day tomorrow. Meet us at Teterboro Airport around five o'clock p.m. with Mona. You can have them both, and me and Mona will take a ride to see Kurt." Geneva barked her orders.

"I don't trust you." There was no other way for me to put it. The last time I was at Teterboro, I almost lost my life.

"Let me tell you something; Mona is your saving grace. I can't hurt my baby girl again."

I felt there was some truth to what Geneva said. I looked at Mona, who had new tears streaming down her face. She was speechless.

"We'll be there—Mona, myself, and my brother A'shai." I guessed Geneva didn't need anything else. The phone went dead.

MONA LISA SUTTON

THIS HAD BEEN one hell of a year, and we had four more months left where anything was likely to happen. We were on our way to Teterboro, and the closer we got, the more my heart rate sped up. The truck was quiet. Mega focused on the road, and A'shai was following in another truck behind us. I saw the bags they brought out. It had to be guns, which made my life flash before my eyes. Had me second guessing and wondering if it was worth it. All these thoughts invaded my mind on the ride.

"Did your father ever text you back?" Mega questioned.

"Not yet. He's not a texter, so it always takes him a while to reply. I looked at the ring camera and noticed his car in the driveway. Whether he texts back or not, we are going over there. If we have to wait for him, so be it." I was determined to get this over with as quickly as possible. It was going to be painful regardless.

"After this, we are going on vacation so we can recharge and continue to get to know each other a little better. I know all of this happened fast, but we got this." Mega took his eyes off the road for a minute, grabbed my hand and kissed it.

"From your lips to God's ears." At this point, he was the only one who could make this right.

"Sometimes I believe in God, but when bad things happen to good people, I question it. I'm probably going to hell anyway, but as long as I do good by the people who love me, I'm cool with that."

Mega had a good heart, but he was jaded from the hard knock life that was given to him.

"I used to feel like I was in hell already. Our thoughts can have our worlds intertwined as one. Having us believe that there is no hope that, in our Father's house, there are many mansions prepared for us. I always wondered why He couldn't do all of that down here. Then I realized the sovereignty of God, that He is the ultimate source of all power, authority, and everything that exists. All I can do is pray that He just helps me maintain while I'm still breathing." There had to be someone in charge who woke us up in the morning.

"I respect that that's your way of thinking about it. Let's see if He comes through for both of us today." Mega put that out in the universe.

My ringtone let me know I had a text.

> DAD:
> I'm home, not going anywhere. Yes, you can come by.

I showed the phone to Mega, and we both were relieved that part was covered.

"You know you don't have to drive me to my dad's house, right? You can get in the truck with A'shai, and I can drive back. I'll be safe. You should really focus on coming home after you do what you are going to do." That needed to be his main concern because jail or death was not something I needed right now.

"Let me peep the scene and feel the energy before I agree to that. All I want is for you to be safe and comfortable while fighting your demons alone."

"That's the only way for me to face them is to do it by myself. Gina is mad I wouldn't let her come. I got this. No longer will they break my soul with their mishaps and shortcomings. At this point, it has nothing to do with me and everything to do with them." I shrugged my shoulders.

"I love the woman you are becoming. This has already changed your life without you even knowing it."

We finally made it to Teterboro. I'd never been to this airport before. All I knew was you had to have money to fly out of these grounds. Celebrities like Mary J. Blige, Missy Elliot, and P. Diddy frequented the tarmac of the runway. It showed how much money and or pull that Geneva and her husband had. There was no turning back now.

Mega entered the code to lift the barrier gate, and we were on our way. I guessed Mega knew where he was going. We were right on time as requested.

"We are here."

We slowed down way before we got to this nice private jet. There was a car waiting.

"Stay right here. As a matter of fact, jump over here on the driver's side. If you see anything crazy, drive off as fast as you can, and I'll meet you at your house."

I didn't want to waste any more time, so I did as I was told. Mega jumped out and ran to the passenger side of the other truck.

I watched as they drove up to the jet. I felt like I was the lookout person, checking my surroundings. My chest tightened up, causing my heartbeat to quicken with anticipation. Mega got out first. A'shai followed with his gun drawn, with what I was sure was adrenaline running through his veins. I felt like I was about to pee on myself from the possibilities of how this could go. So far, I didn't see anything strange, so that was a good sign, I guessed. They both took their time getting to the entrance of the plane. They looked at the little windows to see if they saw any movement.

Honk

The waiting car blew their horn, and it made me jump. Mega and A'shai both had their guns pointed at the vehicle. A window rolled down, and a hand summoned them over. My legs were now shaking, my throat was dry, and hands were sweaty from holding the steering wheel so tight. I couldn't see who was in the car from here, but I was sure it was Geneva or someone who knew where Geneva was. A'shai stood back and watched everything that moved, with his gun ready. This was some real shit I was witnessing.

They talked for a minute, then Mega reached in his pocket and pulled out his phone.

Coco Jones' song "ICU" let me know I was the one Mega was calling.

"What's up?" I tried to calm down enough to get out.

"Geneva is going to follow you to your father's house. I love you. Be safe, and I'll see you later tonight or early morning."

My forehead now rested on the steering wheel, realizing it was a possibility that something could happen to Mega.

"Please be safe and keep me posted. I love you, too, Mega." We hung up, and I put the truck in drive. Through the rearview mirror, I saw the car follow me as soon as I pulled off.

This was the longest drive ever. It was like everybody wanted to cruise in slow motion. Geneva's driver kept up with me as I weaved through the lanes on the highway. We finally made it, and my dad's car was still parked in the driveway. I said a quick prayer, parked, and waited for Geneva to join me. I inserted my key and let us in the house. One thing about my dad was he was very clean and militant when it came to how he wanted his things placed around the house. I watched as Geneva looked around at the place she once called home. We walked around on the first level, looking for my dad, but he must have been upstairs.

"Daddy, you here?" I yelled from the bottom of the steps.

"I'm coming down now."

My dad shouted from wherever he was. Geneva and I both sat down on the couch.

"I was looking for my phone, and I couldn't find it. Call it for…"

My dad stopped dead in his tracks after walking into the living room.

"What are you doing in my house, Geneva?" my dad asked in disbelief, not taking his eyes off the only woman he ever loved.

"Hello, Kurt. You think now is a good time to let our daughter know what really happened?"

Geneva sat back on the couch and crossed her arms.

"You have the audacity to come in here after all these years like we owe you something. What, your career didn't take off like you wanted? Huh? Now you come crawling back, thinking we are supposed to forgive you." My dad spoke with a mix of anger and hurt.

"I'm not here for you. I'm here for my daughter."

"Where were you when your daughter needed you? I'll tell you, Mona. Your mother was whoring in Italy, chasing fame, and giving up pussy as capital."

I cringed at my father's words.

"You still saying that same ol' tired, made-up story. That's what you keep telling yourself? How many times did you rehearse it? Kurt, you can't hurt my feelings anymore. Your words used to cut deep, but I broke out of that prison a long time ago."

Geneva shook her index finger back and forth to signify that it was not going to happen.

"Get the hell out my house. Go back to your other family. We good over here."

My dad got up close with Geneva, and before he could do anything, she pulled out a gun.

"You hit me the last time. Put your hands on me this time, and Mona will lose another parent."

My dad backed up, eyes wide opened from the shock that Geneva had a gun.

"Geneva said she came back for me, but you wouldn't let me go. Did you hit her?" I looked to him for answers.

"She knew it was a mistake. It was something that I couldn't take back. It had already happened."

My dad's evil, bone-chilling stare stayed on Geneva; he didn't even look my way while answering.

"You were no longer the same man I fell in love with. You became bitter. It was almost as if you were jealous that I lived life by my rules. You couldn't stomach the fact that you had to stay home to do lesson plans and grade papers while I had fun creating for some very influential people."

Geneva's hurt started to show a little more through her words.

"You weren't bringing nothing into this house but smokey clothes and liquor breath. We were backed up on our bills, while you went out partying. What did you expect me to do?"

"I expected you to be a man and a husband instead of a coward who didn't want more. We would have still been struggling if I took a job that I hated. Nope. I didn't want that for me or for my daughter. I wanted to show her to never settle for less when you could have so much more."

Geneva did have some qualities of a mother.

"I don't want to hear that shit. You jumped right at the first opportunity to leave. Not only was my love not good enough, but your daughter's love wasn't, either."

My dad's words stung a little.

"Mona, I would have taken you when I first left, but the program didn't allow parents to bring kids. Kurt knew that it was only temporary. He did everything to make it permanent, for his own selfish reasons." Geneva ran it down for me.

"Daddy, you did the same thing she did and kept the cycle going way after she left." My dad started crying.

"That wasn't my intent. I just wanted you to hate her for breaking my heart." He tried holding it in, but the tears flowed.

"It may not have been your intent, but it was my reality and my truth. You have a lot of ground to make up for, and the only way to fix what you broke is to first admit to your wrong doings and seek therapy like we talked about. No longer am I going to be the punching bag for the hurt you don't want to deal with." I'd never been more serious in my life. "This chapter of my life is called free mind so I can be fully present in everyday life." I hope he heard me loud and clear.

"Do you think you can begin to forgive me?" Geneva asked.

My dad started to speak but decided against it.

"Who knows. All I know is that all this time it was you

both who were selfish in raising me. I blamed myself for decades, only to now realize that it was the two of you all along. I need some time to myself, away from the dysfunction of a love that never reached its full potential due to not being equally yoked. None of these things have anything to do with me, so thanks for having me realize that." I got up from the couch.

"Dad, please don't call me until after your first appointment with the therapist. If you don't make that happen, don't even bother to contact me. Geneva, you know how to get back to the airport. Mega better make it home safely because if not, you can forget about getting to know me." With that, I walked out the door, got in the truck, put on my shades, and drove off, finally feeling like my past was behind me in the rearview mirror.

MEGA DAKAR

"I WANNA SEE you talk tough now." I untied Tone's hands and pushed him into the enclosed ring. It was set up like a UFC ring with nowhere to go. He and A'shai were locked in. We were in the sticks of Upstate New York. There was a lot of land and nobody to hear karma bustin' down Tone and Ruby's door. A'shai was jumping back and forth, his eyes stalking Tone like prey. His shirt was off, no gloves, some basketball shorts, and some sneakers.

"I ain't never been scared to fight."

Tone wasn't believable; there was no confidence in his voice.

"You ready to see your son get his ass beat? This is what you should have done when he got Star killed." I looked over to Ruby, who sat tied to a chair. She had front row seats to the bloody massacre that was about to take place. She sat back like she didn't have a care in the world.

We still had her mouth taped; we didn't want her to say anything until we started asking questions.

A'shai started making his way over to Tone, raised hands guarding his face, getting in his slugger stance to go twelve rounds. Tone kept trying to back away, but he didn't have much room to do so. Tone charged at A'shai and caught a knee to his nose. He stumbled back, hitting the gate holding them in. Tone was trying to stop the blood from leaking. He knew he had to gain the advantage or there was hell to pay, more than the payout already given.

"I'm not in a rush. Keep getting up."

A'shai caught Tone with a right hook. He fell to one knee. Before A'shai could get off another hit, Tone punched him right in his balls. A'shai doubled over in pain. Tone got strength from somewhere, jumped up, and close lined A'shai down to the ground.

"You a pussy for that, but it's cool!" I yelled out. Tone looked my way with a wicked red Kool-Aid grin.

"Y'all motherfuckers always thought y'all were better than us. We were good until Ruby brought y'all home."

Tone tried kicking A'shai while he was down, but A'shai caught his foot and yanked him to the ground with him.

"See, you talk too much. I always told you to do less talking and more thinking, but you don't listen."

A'shai was now on top of Tone, giving him body shots to his face, chest, and anywhere that the punch landed. Tone couldn't move. He was trapped by A'shai's body weight and the impact of the blows to his framework.

"It's people like him who make it hard for people like

us." A'shai was out of breath, but he was still pounding on Tone.

Tone had no more fight left in him, but little did he know, it wasn't over. A'shai was the first round; let's see who had next. A'shai didn't stop punching until Tone stopped moving. He was out cold. His face was swollen from the paws that A'shai put on him. Blood was his makeup, and he thought sleeping was going to get him out of what we had next on the agenda. A'shai walked to the gate entrance, and I let him out, giving him a head nod for a job well done. He went straight to the back and brought back Mama and Big Boy, two huge Pitbulls that had muzzles.

They smelled the blood as soon as they entered the farm-like structure and started spazzing out. Ruby's eyes grew bigger at the two large animals that A'shai had on a leash.

"You probably thought we were just going to kill y'all with our guns. Nah, we want every last second of your life to be painful." I kicked over Ruby's chair, and the dogs went ape shit crazy, ready to get at her. This wasn't her fate; this was Tone's ending to his pathetic life. I lifted her back up so she could see the action.

I wanted to make sure to get my money's worth; the dogs were about to get the job done. I got a hold of some chuck steak blood in a plastic pail from a client. I walked in the gated ring and poured it all over Tone's body. It woke him up from getting knocked the hell out. A'shai was now inside with the dogs, and they were fighting to get loose.

We both took the muzzles off the dogs and dropped the leash. We turned around and walked out while the dogs were sinking their sharp teeth through Tone's flesh.

"Please, no… no… oh shit! Oh my God! Tell them to stop." Tone was now pleading for his life. I'd be glad when they finally bit off his lips and left his tongue for dessert. We locked him in with the vultures, giving them their lunch and dinner.

We both stood in front of Ruby, her face bare of her glasses. What people didn't know was she didn't even need them; they were a part of her personality. She was playing a role that became who she was. I wasn't the type of man who hit women, so we had to come up with something different for our caregiver.

First, we wanted to talk to get an understanding of what caused the division and friction amongst the family. If this was anybody else, we wouldn't have considered prolonging the inevitable.

"You always had a lot to say. Let's see what some of your last words are." I ripped the tape from Ruby's mouth, and A'shai grabbed us some chairs. I got comfortable, and A'shai sat down with the back of the chair hitting his chest.

"Why did it have to come to this?" That was the million dollar question of the night.

"You should have brought me some Crown Royal. Where are your manners?" Ruby's crooked smile warranted her teeth to be knocked out. I couldn't take the approach with her though, so I relaxed a little.

"You keep it up, and I won't be as kind as Mega. I'll

push your wig back." There was no love, only hate in A'shai's words and his demeanor.

"You've always been the rebellious one. Untie me from this chair, and I'll whup your ass."

Ruby started shaking the chair, trying to get free. I had to stop A'shai from cutting her loose from her restraints.

"Your death is enough for us, so you better get some shit off your chest before it's lights out." I had to let her know that we weren't going to be here for too much longer. I knew Mona was worried about me, and I was concerned about her, so I had to get home.

"You got a little too big for your britches, thinking you didn't need me anymore. You owe me for all the years that I took care of your ungrateful asses," Ruby disparagingly shared.

"You were all about self. First, it was for the money from the state for us. Then, when you couldn't get that anymore, you used your pussy to get a seat at the table where you didn't belong. It was only a matter of time before that seat became mine. After a while, they were going to see who the heavy hitters were." If I wanted to continue in this life, I was sure our clients wouldn't have minded me running the ship.

"You survived off it, didn't you? Your father should have killed you when he killed your mother."

Ruby's creepy chuckle caused me to back up. I grabbed her by her neck and dangled her in the air as she struggled to breathe.

"Don't worry. You're going to rot in hell with them." I released my grip, and Ruby and the chair fell to the ground.

"A'shai, grab her. Let's go." He dragged her by the legs of the chair on a trail behind us.

We made it across the way, to the industrial furnace designed and made for Ruby and her evil ways. She was hell on earth, so there was no other way for her to go out. A'shai and I stopped right in front of the cremation chamber. I turned it on, and it roared with power, signaling that it was now on and ready for use. Ruby began kicking and screaming once she came to from all the bumps and bruises she took getting over here.

"Just shoot me. All you have to do is shoot meeeeeeee."

I opened the door while A'shai cut the rope that Ruby was tied up with. I hurried and grabbed one arm and leg, and A'shai grabbed the others. Ruby was going wild, but we were able to get her up to the entrance to throw her in.

"Pleaseeeeeee!" Ruby pleaded, trying to kick and bang her way out of the now closed chamber.

"You should have thought about that before your loyalty became a weapon to our life!" I yelled for her to hear me. "You can do the honors," I said to A'shai once it was time.

A'shai pressed the red circle button, and the machine came to life. You could instantly feel the heat coming from the big compactor of death.

"Oh my God... Nooooooooo!" I wished we could see Ruby's face, but hearing her cry out was like music to my ears.

A'shai and I looked at each other, satisfied with the outcome.

"Money," A'shai mouthed.

"Power," I followed up.

"Respect," A'shai echoed.

"Is the key to life," I finished.

We walked out, leaving everything for the clean-up crew.

MONA LISA SUTTON

ONE YEAR Later

NO WAY!

I looked at the two lines on the First Response stick.

I was surprised it didn't happen sooner with the way Mega kept my legs wrapped around him. I sat on the toilet with thoughts of this past year on my mind. I had one successful event under my belt at the Mets. I hosted a night of black excellence which was displayed in each painting. The networking I did at that event made me a household name. So many celebrities were hitting me up, asking me to make them custom paintings for their billion-dollar homes. Picturesque was even booked. No longer were we chasing talent; they were now coming to us.

With all these great things happening, Mega and I got a little unraveled in this thing called love and life. I ordered my dress a few months ago for this special night and couldn't even fit it, which caused me to take a pregnancy test, realizing I'd been so busy that I hadn't noticed mother nature's absence. I'd always been a big girl, so it didn't even dawn on me. I just needed to get through the night and worry about this problem at a later date. Tonight was important, and I couldn't be more proud to share this moment.

I wrapped the pregnancy test up in a paper towel and put it in the nightstand on my side of the bed.

I wished I could share the news with my dad, but he still hadn't come around. That told me he still hadn't gone to see the therapist. That was a little concerning, but my life was finally moving in the right direction, and I wasn't going to let my dad take that from me. I prayed, one day, it would get better. My dad was no longer my priority.

Geneva and I were still getting to know one another. We tried to talk at least once a month. She kept asking when she could come to visit. Maybe she could, for the baby shower, if she was lucky.

Ding dong.

The doorbell rang, and I hurried to answer it. I already knew who it was; it was my girl, here to save the day.

"You knew who to call. I got you covered. You better be glad I got a stylist on speed dial." Gina came in looking snatched to the gods from head to toe. She was Met Gala ready.

"Why are you just trying on your dress anyway? Isn't that against the girl code or some shit?" A'shai came in behind Gina.

"Lay off my girl, yo." I could always count on Mega to

show up for me. He walked up smelling good in his Dior Sauvage cologne. His black and gold suit jacket fit him perfectly, hugging his arms, and his pants were fitted around his toned thighs.

"If it wasn't for you, I wouldn't even be going to this lame gala." A'shai's abstract black designer tux didn't look too bad on him either.

"Nobody is forcing you, so chill. I got a blunt waiting for you in the cave. You know they are about to take a long time." I gave Mega a love punch as he and A'shai walked by, talking about us like we weren't standing right here.

"Bitchhhh! Did you take it?" Gina was so loud.

"Damn, girl. Be quiet." I helped her with my items and led the way up to the room. As soon as I dropped the items on the bed, I reached in the nightstand. As soon as Gina looked up and saw what it read, she couldn't contain her excitement.

"Oh my God, oh my God! I told you! I fucking told you!" Gina was jumping up and down. I wanted her to calm down before Mega and A'shai came up here.

"Girl, shut up. I'm waiting until after the gala to tell Mega. I want him to enjoy his night. I don't want to take his shine." He deserved this moment. His painting was being showcased during the Met Gala this year.

"I'm gonna be an auntie, an auntie." Gina started dancing, still singing her auntie song.

It made me smile to know that I had such a supportive friend. I was where I was because of her, both professionally and personally. We were two Black girls, thriving, being the bosses we were born to be. Both of us had trauma, but we learned that it didn't define us. Our childhoods weren't easy, but we sure didn't do bad for ourselves.

Gina got me together to look good alongside my man. I looked at myself in the mirror, noticing the weight gain but not caring. This was what most people would consider healthy weight. I didn't know if that was a thing, but this was the healthiest I'd ever been.

"Mega is going to be so happy."

"Happy about what?" Mega and A'shai walked into the room, ready to go.

Gina grabbed the paper towel and test along with all her other beauty supplies.

"It's a surprise." I kissed Mega, hoping it would take his mind off wanting to know the answer.

"This ain't no porn set, so y'all need to get on with all that," Gina said with a scrunched-up face.

"There you go again, all in their business. What I tell you about that?" A'shai smacked Gina on her butt.

"You tell me a lot of things. That doesn't mean I listen." Gina stuck out her tongue.

"I'm going to make sure you hear me this time, don't worry." A'shai shook his head up and down with the understanding that he would get the last laugh.

"What's the name of y'all reality show? That shit needs to be on BET." I wasn't lying though. They went back and forth like they were on camera to entertain.

"Man, let's go." Mega had, had enough. I ran to the bathroom and got dressed quickly with Gina's help.

My new normal was something I had to get used to. Old habits sometimes took a lifetime to break. With both Ruby and Tone eliminated, I could say it became a little easier. I was able to put my focus elsewhere, like on the shop and giving Mona the best that I had. I guessed it was all worth it in the end. Unfortunately, I lost some people in the battle, but I seemed to be winning the war. I would never get caught slipping because I'd quickly show the opps how it was really goin' down. I'd always be ready so I wouldn't have to get ready.

The Met Gala investigators were still snooping around. The last Mona told me is that they were still going through evidence that they collected on the scene. It'd been over a year, if they hadn't found anything by now, I doubted they would. Mona's painting alone brought in way more money to the Mets than the Maurizio Contini painting would have.

I didn't expect that to happen, but I was glad it did because it took the blame off Mona and Picturesque a little. It was billed as pending investigation in the media, and no follow-up had been given.

"Are you nervous?" Mona brought me out of my thoughts on our drive to the museum.

I wasn't nervous about people seeing the painting. I was nervous about something way bigger.

"As long as you are with me, how could I be nervous?" I looked over at her on the passenger side.

"I see you trying to get some tonight." Mona eyed me, knowing she was the one who was trying to get some. Her hands gliding across my chest told me all I needed to know.

"I was getting some either way." I guided her hand to my shaft.

We pulled up to the designated area and let the valet do its thing. I thought Mona's event had a lot of people. There was a lot of star power out tonight, and we still were the best-looking couple. We took pictures, laughed, and enjoyed the pre-festivities before we went in for the night. This time, I was being asked the questions. The spotlight was on me, and I didn't like that. This would probably be my first and last event. If they wanted my paintings, they could buy them, but there would be no major events on my behalf.

The whole night, we chilled and took in the scenery. We all had a drink in our cup, except for Mona. She said she wanted to be sober to get the whole experience of me showing my painting to the world. That meant a lot to me, knowing she was excited to show me off. There was such a thing as life after death. A part of me died when I lost Mya, but the new me came alive when I met Mona. I didn't think it was possible, but here I stood.

"Please welcome Mr. Mega Dakar." I got up from my seat and grabbed Mona's hand for her to go to the podium with me.

"Thank you, thank you. I'm not much of a talker, so this will be really short." I didn't let go of Mona's hand. I looked over at her, and she was smiling with love in her eyes. I continued.

"I fell in and out of love with painting, not realizing that it would lead me to this very moment in time. This painting is dedicated to this beautiful woman that I'm holding on to. She is the reason why I stand here today, before you, sharing something I didn't know was a gift. She constantly reminds me of the king in me, even when I have the slightest doubt." I paused for a minute to make sure I had everybody's attention, including the future Mrs. Mona Lisa Dakar.

"Miss Mona Lisa Sutton, will you marry me?" I hoped that this would be my last time asking someone that. The 3.29 carat IVS2 cushion cut, diamond halo engagement ring shined through Mona's eyes.

"Yes! Yes! I'll marry you." Mona jumped up and down. I took the ring out and put it on her finger.

"I love you." I grabbed her up and planted kisses all over her face.

"We love you, too." I wasn't sure who this 'we' was she was talking about.

"We?" I looked on for an answer.

"I'm pregnant." Mona's glow told me all I needed to know.

I dropped to my knees in front of everyone and kissed Mona's stomach.

"Thanks for making me one of the happiest men alive." I finally felt like my life was complete.

A'SHAI BLAZE

"Yo, y'all baby gonna have a big ass head," I joked, happy that one of us got the happy ending.

"Let's fight, yo." Mega and I both got in our slap boxing stance, laughing and joking, realizing for the first time, we could finally breathe.

While Mega was done with the streets, I didn't think it would be that easy for me. The power I held over people while death was knocking resonated with me. I looked forward to blood leaking and the pleas that came along with it. That was how I was built; I was manufactured that way by my reality. I was willing to give this new life a chance, but as soon as I needed to feed the beast, I was going hunting. The night was coming to an end. I couldn't wait to have my dick in Gina's butt as she drained me dry.

"Shai, you need to get home. Don't you have your big

test tomorrow?" Gina brought me out of my sexual thoughts of her.

"You didn't tell me you chose a date, bro'." Mega looked at me confused.

"I didn't want to take your shine. It's no biggie." It was only a test. If I passed, I passed. If not, I was cool with that, too. I looked at Gina, shaking my head.

"My bad." Gina was sincere, but I was going to have to teach her to keep her mouth closed.

I was set to take the New Jersey Real Estate Exam the following morning. School had never been my thing, but I was trying. The course wasn't bad, and all I saw was dollar signs, so that motivated me to really pay attention. I even started looking at houses in Paterson that I could fix up and sell. That was where I was going to start, and once I got my feet wet, I was going to branch off into larger homes where the white people spent money.

"Make it up to me later." My eyes told Gina all she needed to know.

"Ewww... Bye." Mona rolled her eyes, giving Gina a hug. We were saying our goodbyes while waiting for our cars to pull up.

"Call me as soon as you are done taking the test." Mega and I embraced. "I'm proud of you." The feeling was mutual.

Vroom! Vroom! Skrt!!

Red, white, and blue lights flashed as six black unmarked cars surrounded us. I wasn't sure what was going on, but my hand was on my gun just in case. They looked to be cops, so I had to play this right. My heart was racing.

I wasn't scared; I just needed to know what the deal was. They all seemed to get out of the cars at the same time. Badges were around their necks. They rushed toward all of us. They made their way right to me, hands on their weapons. The leader of the pack held up a paper. From a quick glance, it looked like a warrant.

"Are you A'shai Blaze?" I looked this dude up and down as he asked a question he already knew the answer to.

"It depends on who's asking," I spat with fire.

"Detective Montez Dawkins, and behind me is my team. We have a warrant for your arrest for the disappearance of Julius Rivers." I wasn't sure who he was talking about until he continued. "Ms. Sutton, we have now found our suspect and are closer to finding out what happened to the Maurizio Contini painting. We were wondering how the painting went missing until we figured out that the security guard was missing. Your blood puts you at the scene." Detective Dawkins was very confident in what he was saying.

My lawyer would have to do the talking for me. I put my hands behind my back to make it easy for them. I looked to Mega as a crowd started to gather to see what was happening. He already knew what time it was. We planned for shit like this. What had me tripping was wondering where I went wrong. I always covered my tracks. Shit didn't make sense. I had time to add all this shit up while I awaited my fate.

BLANK CANVAS OF YOU SPIN-OFF

Blank Canvas of You Spin-Off

She was building a name from the pieces they left behind.

He was learning how to live without the noise that once defined him.
Gina Thompson and A'Shai Blaze never disappeared from each other's orbit.
They were always close, always familiar, always unfinished.
What changed wasn't distance. It was timing.
What started as comfort without commitment slowly demanded more.
More honesty.
More risk.
More than the safety of bodies meeting without hearts involved.
Their connection lives in contradiction.
Laughter under pressure.
Touch where pain still lives.
Truth spoken in the kind of silence that can either save you or swallow you whole.
They weren't trying to save each other.
Love was never the plan. It was the consequence.
Because healing doesn't always come from holding on.
Sometimes it comes from breaking beautifully.
This is their necessity.
Their truth.
Their Stone Cold Love Story.

Read Here: https://amzn.to/4qXfHbY

www.ingramcontent.com/pod-product-compliance
Lightning Source LLC
LaVergne TN
LVHW011807060526
838200LV00053B/3684